Caitlin's Country

Jeanne McNamara

ISBN-13:978-1497524958

Printed in U.S.A.
1stbooks – rev. 2/28/2000
This edition first printing 2014

For my daughter Amy, my angel

CHAPTER 1

Long Distance

"Why don't you think about coming to live in Australia with me?"

I put down the phone with my father's words ringing in my ears. Australia? It was so far away from Boston, and my parents had been divorced for years. My father was almost a stranger to me, and his land was a foreign country.

"What did your dad have to say, dear?"

Aunt Natalie was in on the conspiracy, of course. She knew why my father had called from Sydney, Australia. Aunt Natalie and Uncle Tim had three children of their own. They were so kind to me after I lost my mother, but I had taken one of their bedrooms when I came to stay with them, which must have been a nuisance. "Dad wants me to go and live with him for a while," I said, quietly.

"What do you think about that idea?" Aunt Natalie asked.

"I don't know. I've never even visited there."

"Well, you know you will always have a home here with us." Aunt Natalie reached for a cookie-cutter in the drawer. We were in her white New England kitchen where she was forever baking and rinsing dishes and picking up toys.

"What is he like?" I asked.

"Your dad? Don't you remember him?"

I shook my head. "He sounds young on the phone. What does he do - for a job, I mean?"

"He used to be a journalist." Aunt Natalie carefully pressed the cookie-cutter into the dough. She was a pretty brunette like my mother had been. "You could go to Australia for the summer. If you don't like it there, you can come back to Boston in time to start school in the fall."

It was a good thought. I was fifteen and in the tenth grade. I could come back to America if I found I disliked living with my father. After all, I had moved all the way from Texas to be with Aunt Natalie, my mother's younger sister. In some ways, Boston was foreign - the weather, and the way people talked and dressed. "Do you know why he went back to Australia?" I asked.

"Your mother said Australians don't make good migrants," Aunt Natalie said. "Life is easy Down Under, and your dad missed the gum trees or something."

"Could I buy a return ticket? I would feel better if I knew I could come home any time I wanted."

Aunt Natalie set aside the cookie tray. "You don't have to go at all, if you don't want to."

The telephone intruded again. Aunt Natalie reached to answer it. "It's your dad again."

I took the phone. "Well," the male voice asked, "have you decided?"

I could not help giggling. If I knew nothing else about my father, I knew now that he was impulsive.

Uncle Tim spread a map of the world out on the dining-room table. We all gathered around him to look at Australia. Uncle Tim was a college professor and he loved an audience. "It is as far away from Boston as you can get," he explained, "before you start coming back home to America."

"Is Australia an island?" I asked.

My three small cousins - Marybeth, Alicia, and Peter - stared at the map with big, round eyes. "Australia is the world's largest island," Uncle Tim said, "and the smallest continent, whichever way you like to look at it. It will be winter by the time you arrive in Sydney."

I was dismayed. "Another winter?"

"But it won't be as severe as this," Uncle Tim said. "You will need a passport and a visa to travel there, of course."

"Even though my father is an Australian?"

"Yes, but you shouldn't have any problem. If I were you, I would just take some clothes and a few personal things that you can't do without. Leave everything else here until you decide what you're going to do about the future."

"I wonder what the schools are like," I said.

"To be honest, Caitlin," Uncle Tim said, "I've already had a word with your dad about that. He thinks you might be happier at a private school."

"Not boarding school?" I asked.

"No, but a lot of kids go to private schools in Sydney."

I felt my stomach sink, the way it did when I was in a situation that I could not control. "I would rather go to public school."

Uncle Tim closed the atlas. "You'll soon make new friends, wherever you are."

That night, before I went to sleep, I propped myself up on the pillows and carefully turned the pages of my parents' wedding album. It was now almost six months since my mother had died in an automobile accident in Dallas. She looked so beautiful on her wedding day and my father was young and tall. Of course, he was older now, though he sounded like a boy on the phone.

I put aside the photo album and gazed around the room. It was really my cousin Peter's room, decorated with blue and red wallpaper. Sadly, I remembered my pretty pink bedroom at home, where my mother had let me choose the colors and the furnishings. Of course, Boston was not my home. I had no home, not without my mother. I had nothing to lose by taking a chance on my dad.

~ ~ ~

A month later, my cousins were helping me pack my bags for the plane trip to Australia. I took care with my hand-luggage, making sure I had everything I needed for the long flight.

At the last minute, Uncle Tim said, "I've decided to come with you as far as Los Angeles, so that I can see you on board."

Aunt Natalie said, "I think you should carry your spring coat with you, Caitlin. You might get cold on the plane."

"Do you want this took?" Peter asked, holding up my large teddy bear.

"I don't think I can take Teddy to Australia," I told him. "You had better keep him for me. There is no way I can pack my whole life into two bags."

Ever since I had decided to go to Australia, Aunt Natalie had looked worried. Now, her eyes filled with tears. "You have to take what is important to you."

"Everything will be all right, Aunty," I said. "I am going to my father."

"I know, dear." Aunt Natalie managed to smile. "But we will miss you."

"Look on the bright side. Peter can have his room back again."

"Will you write to us every week and call at least once a month?"

"Of course."

"You won't be driving, will you?" my aunt asked. "You know they drive on the wrong side of the road in Australia."

"I won't have a car," I reminded her. "Anyway, I'd be too scared to drive on the other side of the road."

Aunt Natalie went into the bathroom for a tissue to wipe her eyes. When she came back, I was in tears, too.

CHAPTER 2

The Flight

The flight to Sydney was not the way I had imagined at all. I had expected to feel important and glamorous, like a movie star. Instead, the plane was filled with noisy families, babies and young children, and the flight attendants, though polite, were busy and preoccupied.

Still, it was nice at night when they handed out blankets and pillows and turned down the lights. It felt so cozy, I managed to get a few hours of sleep, though I was sitting next to a mother with two small children.

Coming into Sydney Airport, the first thing I saw was the blue water of Port Jackson and then the Sydney Harbor Bridge and the Opera House. I had seen these places on television, and it felt unreal to be looking at them from the window of a plane. It was almost too overwhelming as I sank back into my seat and tightened my seat-belt.

When we left the plane, I lined up at the Immigration Desk with the other foreign passengers. A uniformed official looked over my American passport and asked, cheerfully, "Are you visiting your family and having a little holiday, love?"

A young passenger in boots and a cowboy hat helped me collect my suitcase. He was a Texan and I felt homesick when he said, with a smile, "Have a good one!"

Customs was easy, too. I was ready to open my bags and let the Customs Officer inspect everything inside, but all he said was, "Are you carrying any milk products or fruit, miss?"

"No, sir," I replied.

"Caitlin?"

I had been so busy with my luggage, I almost forgot to look for my father as I came out of the Customs Hall. But he had found me. "Are you all right?" David Pritchard asked, smiling at me. "Do you have everything? Just the two bags?"

"Yes, please," I said, shyly, looking up at my father. He was still tall and slim, casually dressed in blue jeans and a denim jacket. He made no attempt to hug or kiss me and I was grateful for that. I hardly knew any more about this man than about the other people milling around us in the airport. Listening to the Australian voices, I realized how different I must sound with my American accent.

"Are you hungry?" my father asked. "We have a fair way to go."

"I had breakfast on the plane," I said.

Leaving the airport cart behind in the terminal, my father carried my heavy bags across to the parking lot, swinging them into the back of an old yellow station-wagon. "This side," he said.

I felt myself blushing. I had forgotten that the steering-wheel was on the other side of the car. "I suppose there are lots of things to get used to."

My father smiled again. "You'll soon settle in. I don't know if Aunt Natalie told you, but I don't live in Sydney."

"Where do you live?" I asked.

"About forty miles away in Emu Plains, out in the sticks."

"The sticks?"

"The back-blocks," he explained.

"Aunt Natalie said you were a journalist."

"I used to be. I'm in the antique business now."

My father started the car and I stared out of the window, absorbing these two pieces of information. He was not the successful journalist I had imagined. He was a dealer in second-hand wares, and he lived in a place with a strange name. "Where is Emoo Plains?" I asked.

"Emu," he corrected me. "Not far, once we get

on the freeway."

At least there was a freeway. It was disconcerting, though, driving on the left-hand side of the road, but not so unsettling as the fact that my father wore jeans, drove a dilapidated car and had a questionable job. I could not help thinking about the second-hand dealer who came to the house to buy my mother's china dishes after she died, offering fifty cents for each lovely piece.

"Do you see that house, Caitlin?"

I looked ahead of me to the house at the end of the street. "The red brick one?"

"Well," my father drawled, turning the wheel, "that's not it. See that house there? That's not it, either."

Finally, we stopped in front of a small stone bungalow. "See that house there?"

I decided to play the game. "Yes."

My father grinned. "That's it."

The little house looked a bit neglected. The picket fence needed repairs and the front door had been roughly painted several times over, in different colors. I could almost hear my mother, a real estate agent, assessing the property. She would have called the house a "fixer-upper." But I said, politely, "It looks very nice."

My father was unloading the luggage from the station-wagon. "I bought this place about two years ago. It was built by convicts."

I gathered up my coat. "Convicts?"

"I don't suppose you know any of Australia's history. The colony was settled by convicts and soldiers from Britain about two hundred years ago. The story goes that this is one of the houses they built out here."

Inside the cottage, the narrow hallway was gloomy, with dark wooden floors and a couple of framed pictures hanging on the walls. Carrying my belongings, my father led me into a small room at the front of the house. "I thought I would put you in here. This room has a working fireplace. Unfortunately, we don't have central heating."

I looked around the bedroom where I would be spending at least one semester. The rough plaster walls were painted dark green and the pine wardrobe, dressing-table and bed looked like antiques. But the white comforter on the bed and the drapes at the window were fresh and pretty. "A friend of mine helped me decorate it for you," my father said.

I realized he was waiting for my reaction. I said, hurriedly, "This is great."

"I had to replace all the floor boards in the house.

The original timber was eaten by white-ants - termites, you would call them."

I put my coat and purse down on the bed and instinctively went to the window. Through the little panes of glass, I could see the tree-covered hills in the distance - the Blue Mountains, I knew the forest was called - and in the foreground the tiled roofs of other, newer houses. "Our house was the first to be built here," my father said, "so of course we have the best view. Do you want to see the rest of the house?"

"Oh, yes," I said, trying to sound more cheerful than I felt.

As we walked about the cottage, my father pointed to the light switches high up on the walls. "Don't forget, there are 240 volts running through the wires - more dangerous than 110 volts. Down is 'on' and up is 'off.' That hatch in the wall is where the convict-servants used to pass the meals through to the family. I moved the kitchen into the main house when I was renovating."

I followed my father about, listening to his stories. I could see that my new life was going to be a bigger challenge than I expected. No one had told me that he lived in a tired old house built in the nineteenth century. At least the bathroom had been updated, though the colors were from the 1950's - green and pink. My mother had taught me that everything looked brighter after a good night's sleep, and so I tried to stay positive.

I understood that my father was doing his best to make me feel welcome. I could not help liking him. But as he showed me around what was now my home, too, I noticed there were no pictures of my mother on display. He had a framed photograph of me beside his bed, taken when I was about six years old.

CHAPTER 3

Emu Plains

"Where is the high school from here?" I asked, gazing around the old-fashioned kitchen. A scrubbed-pine dresser took the place of built-in cabinets, and a wood stove was pressed against one wall. Incongruously, opposite that stood a modern electric range and a stainless-steel sink.

I sat down at the pine table. "You drink tea, don't you?" my father asked, filling the electric kettle.

"Mom and I always had tea together," I said.

"Good. We need to talk about your school. I would rather you went to a private school, if you don't hate the idea too much. Tennyson College is not far from here. It is a small school and only for girls."

I swallowed. "Back home, I went to public school."

"I know, but I thought it might be easier for you to settle in to the College."

"Won't a private school be expensive?"

"That is not your worry," my father said, "but I have to tell you that they wear a uniform. Most schools here do."

I felt my throat starting to ache. Oh, to be back in Dallas or Boston where people lived in normal houses and went to public school in blue jeans. "What kind of uniform?"

"Brown, I think." My father's voice was matter-of-fact. "I have already talked to the headmistress. They are looking forward to having a 'Yank' at their school."

The most beautiful perfume was wafting through the back door, and my father had put a plate of little cream cakes on the table. I said, as steadily as I could, "I am not a Yankee. I am a Texan."

He gave his ready smile. "You might have to explain that to Australians. Most of them don't understand the difference between the North and the South."

I knew I should be more enthusiastic, especially when my father was trying to make me feel at home. At least, that is what my mother would have told me. "Do you have any pets?" I asked.

"I have a cat who adopted me," my father said. "Sebastian is out the back somewhere."

"At home, we never let our cat outside."

"It is very quiet around here. There aren't many cars, and no coyotes. Where is your cat now?"

"I left Tiffany with Aunt Natalie," I said. "She

would have had to go into quarantine to come to Australia and Tiffany is too old for that."

My father sat down at the table. "What do you want to call me? If you aren't comfortable with Dad, you can call me David."

"Dad is fine," I said.

He looked pleased and began spooning lots of sugar into his cup. "What did you want to do for the rest of the day?"

I said, carefully, "Is this Monday or Tuesday?"

"It is Tuesday. You lost a day coming across the Pacific Ocean."

"Don't you have to go back to work?"

"My shop is closed on Tuesdays. Would you like to see it? We could do a quick tour of the place, then pick up hamburgers for lunch."

"Do you have hamburgers here?" I asked.

"And fries. We call them chips. The hamburgers aren't quite the same as they are in America. You will have to try fish-and-chips some time, too."

"I can't. I am vegetarian."

"Are you?" My father did not sound surprised. "I will have to remember that."

I said, "Can I ask you something - something

personal?"

"Ask away."

"Did you ever get married again, after you and Mom were divorced?"

My father reached for a cream cake. "Actually, I am planning to get married in a few months. Her name is Enid. I am sure you will like her."

Why would I like her, I asked myself? Right then, I knew I would have to find out when the spring semester started in Boston. I could not live here in this tiny cottage with my father and someone called Enid. A step-mother had not been part of the plan. "Aunt Natalie didn't tell me about that."

"Aunt Natalie doesn't know yet."

While my father was talking to someone on the phone, I went outside to look around the back yard. The day was sunny and fair, and quite warm - fall weather in New South Wales. The garden was no more than a wide strip of untidy lawn sloping down to a rickety wooden fence. Beyond that, a clump of spindly willow trees bent over a dried-up creek bed. The land on the other side of the creek was vacant and covered with thick bracken.

"The neighbor next door says she used to see wallabies hopping around when she first came here."

My father had come to stand beside me on the porch. "What are wallabies?" I asked.

"Small kangaroos."

"Are there any koalas?"

"We will have to go to the zoo to see those, but a spiny ant-eater came into my front yard once, when the weather was very dry."

I looked at my father. "When you said your house was built by convicts, did you mean criminals?"

"Petty criminals. They were sent out from the old country in the 1800's, for things like shop-lifting. Some of them were given land around here. You will probably learn about the convicts in school."

"I didn't know Australia was a colony."

"It used to be - like the American Colonies."

"Was this a farm house?"

"This place was probably built for an overseer of some kind. The farm house used to be over there." My father pointed across the creek. "They tore it down when they built the new shopping center in the 1970's. No one had lived there for years."

I shivered. "I hope there aren't any ghosts."

"I have never seen any," he said, solemnly. "I did find a couple of old graves on the other side of the creek. I like to imagine they were pioneers."

These days, when anyone talked about graves and cemeteries, I thought about my mother's funeral and the green canopy sheltering the mourners from the rain while the earth wept, too. My father said, as though reading my thoughts, "I wish I could have been at your mother's funeral."

I did not answer him. I looked towards the willow trees at the bottom of the garden and I could see a small black cat poking about in the grass. "Is that your cat?"

"That is Sebastian," my father said. "He likes to play down there. My land ends at the fence. The rest is Crown land - something like Corps land in Texas. No one will care if you want to explore, but be careful. There could be snakes even at this time of year, and watch out for spiders. Funnel webs are deadly."

In Dallas, people worried about getting "mugged" and traffic accidents. Emu Plains was a suburb of Sydney, yet it seemed more like the outback. Here, danger came from power-switches and wildlife. Again, as though sensing my thoughts, my father said, "I know it seems wild, but we are on the edge of the National Forest. Most native animals are protected by law, even snakes."

"We have lots of snakes in Texas," I said.

CHAPTER 4

New School

Dad and I sat together in his station-wagon outside the gates of Tennyson College. He was wearing jeans, as usual, and he had a set of chairs loaded into the back of the station-wagon like a delivery driver. "I didn't want to go to an all-girls' school," I told him.

"I've heard girls do better in schools without boys," my father replied, calmly.

I took another look at the red brick building behind the wrought iron gates. "I've always gone to a co-ed' school. This isn't a boarding school, is it?"

"No, I think it used to be a convent for Church of England nuns."

"What are Church of England nuns?"

"Never mind." My father opened the car door. "Let's go and have a look."

Reluctantly, I climbed out of the car, my shoes crunching on the gravel driveway. The portico over the front door of the school was very formal, almost old-world, not the way I expected a school to look. Inside, the foyer surrounded visitors with heavy polished wood and brass, and I was glad I was wearing what my mother called a "church" dress. But my father seemed to be doing fine in his jeans as he confidently gave his name to the receptionist, his voice echoing around the paneled walls. It was after nine o'clock and the students had probably gone to class. I could hear the muffled sound of girlish voices down the hallway.

Miss Shock, the middle-aged headmistress, took us into her office. She said, kindly, "I was very sorry to hear about your mother, Caitlin. We always keep a few places open for girls who come from abroad."

"Thank you, ma'am," I said.

"You may call me Miss Shock. If you have trouble assembling the uniform by Monday, the frock you are wearing will be quite suitable on your first day."

My father said, "Coming from the States, Caitlin isn't used to wearing a uniform, Miss Shock."

"Tennyson girls are proud of their uniform," Miss Shock said, "and it is a requirement of the school. I don't allow my girls to wear jewelry, but if you have pierced ears, you may wear studs. Do you play the piano, Caitlin?"

"No, ma'am."

"What a pity." Miss Shock straightened her glasses. "Before we go any further, I must tell you about our History Day next week. At this school, we are very proud of our country's heritage."

"Well," my father said, as we left Miss Shock's office, "what did you think of the school?"

"It looks all right," I admitted. "Did you go to a private school?"

My father was searching in his pockets for his car keys. "No, I went to a state school in the bush - public school."

I could not help smiling. "Did you notice Miss Shock called my dress a frock?"

"I did get the impression Miss Shock might be a tad old-fashioned."

I looked back over my shoulder at the school gates. "Do you really think this is the right place for me?"

"Yes, I think you need a soft place to land after all you have been through."

~~~

"Enid," my father said, "this is Caitlin. Caitlin, this is Enid."

"Pleased to meet you, ma'am," I said.

We were in Enid Durham's house in Glenbrook in the lower Blue Mountains. The house had a large living-room with a galley kitchen at one end and a bedroom at the other. It smelled of beeswax and something that reminded me of my grandmother's house in Texas. Enid was younger than I had pictured her. She wore hardly any make-up and her auburn hair was tied with a green ribbon.

"How do you do, Caitlin? You are a little Yank, aren't you?"

My father said, quickly, "'Yank' has a different meaning to Americans, Enid."

I frowned at him. "It doesn't matter, Dad."

"Of course it doesn't," Enid said. "How did you enjoy your visit to Tennyson College?"

"It was fine, thank you," I said.

"I went there when I was a girl. It wasn't half so posh as it is now. I am pleased to hear they accepted a shopkeeper's daughter."

My father winked at me. "Of course they did. Anyway, they see me as an antique dealer."

We had picked up fish-and-chips for dinner on our way to Enid's house. "I will just have chips," I said, when my father was placing the order.

He looked at me. "I will get you a salad as well."

At Enid's house, my father unpacked our dinner, while his fiancé spread a red gingham cloth on the kitchen table. "Will you be helping David in the shop, Caitlin?" she asked.

Before I could answer, my father said, "Caitlin will have enough to do keeping up with her school work."

Enid put a bottle of ketchup in the middle of the table labeled "Tomato Sauce." "Why are you acting like a mother hen, David? Do you think I am going to say something that might upset your daughter?"

My father went to the refrigerator. "We will have to overlook Enid's manners, Caitlin. She is an artist and all artists are eccentric."

I was still feeling shy with my father's fiancé. "What kind of artist?" I managed to ask.

"I am a painter," Enid said. "This used to be my mother's house and art gallery. The gallery is just through that door. I'll take you to see her collection, if you're interested."

I thought about my mother and the way she loved collecting paintings and pieces of local sculpture. "Thank you, ma'am."

"Please call me Enid."

"Well," my father said, "let's tuck in."

I could not help giggling. Enid smiled, too. "That means let's eat. I grew up in the Blue Mountains," she went on. "When I first came home from England, I wasn't sure I wanted to move back here, but it has worked out well, hasn't it, David?"

"Very well."

"I only came back to Australia because I needed to settle my mother's estate. In London, I thought the world was my oyster. When I arrived back in Sydney, I didn't want to get off the plane."

"Then you met me," my father said, lightly.

"I met David when I was selling some of my mother's furniture," Enid added. "By the way, did you buy the school uniform?"

"Everything except the apron for domestic science," my father said. "The girls make their own in class."

Enid smiled. "I can't believe they still do that."

"I can't sew," I said, "and I need a long dress to wear on History Day."

"There are lots of vintage clothes at David's shop. You should be able to find something there."

"What about the plate?" my father asked. "Miss Shock said Caitlin has to bring a plate to school on History Day."

"She meant a plate of food, silly," Enid said. "Why don't you make some pikelets?"

I was beginning to feel more at ease. "What are pikelets?"

"Little pancakes you eat with butter or jam."

"Let's make some for us as well," my father suggested.

CHAPTER 5

The New Girl

After my first week in Australia, if I had been asked to list three things about my new home, I would have said, "Dust, food that tastes as good as it looks, and friendly people."

But my father still seemed worried as he said good-bye to me at the gate of Tennyson College. "Are you sure you don't want me to pick you up this afternoon? I could try to get away from the shop."

I felt about twelve in my school uniform: brown plaid skirt, navy blazer, and of all things, lace-up shoes. I said, as cheerfully as I could, "I'll be fine, Dad. I am used to walking home from school."

"Are you? It is only a few blocks," he added, as though reassuring himself.

A petite, dark-haired girl sat next to me in my first class, which was history. She gave me a gentle handshake. "I am Ann Engels. I'll bet you don't know anything about Australian history."

I smiled. "Not a thing."

"It's about Captain Cook discovering Australia and the explorers crossing the Blue Mountains. Where abouts in America did you live?"

I was aware that other girls in the classroom were listening, too. "In Dallas, Texas," I said.

"Where the Dallas Cowboys come from? That must have been exciting."

The girl behind me leaned forward. "Do you know how to line dance?"

Other girls joined in. "Have you seen Brad Pitt?"

"Have you been to Disney World?"

"Did you have a boy-friend in America?"

I shook my head to all these questions.

"Kids in America don't wear school uniforms, do they?" someone said.

"Some schools have uniforms," I said.

"I like your accent," Ann said.

"I like yours."

"Do I have an accent?" Ann sounded surprised. "What sports do you play?"

"I swim, and I was learning to play golf when--- when I left."

"I hurt my knee playing netball." Ann grimaced. "Now I can't do any sports, and I have to wear this wretched bandage all the time." I had already noticed the bandage on Ann's knee. "Here comes Mr. Mackerel. He's the history teacher."

Mr. Mackerel put his books down on the desk. "Good-morning, everyone."

"Good-morning, Mr. Mackerel," the girls chorused.

Ann whispered, "Don't you think he looks like a fish?"

At lunch time, Ann tucked her arm through mine as though we were already good friends. "I'll show you the way to the refectory."

"The cafeteria?" I guessed.

"Take a salad sandwich and milk," Ann instructed. "That's what I always have."

In the refectory, I picked up a sandwich in plastic wrap and a carton of milk from the counter and followed Ann and the other girls to a table. The walls of the cafeteria were paneled in dark wood and the ceiling was decorated with ornate plaster, giving the room a hushed tone. "Do you ever have school dances?" As soon as I had spoken, I realized how tactless that was to ask Ann about dancing, with her knee injury.

Ann was not concerned. "Brebner Academy is

sort of our 'brother' school. We have dances with them every month. Did you hear what Mr. Mackerel said about History Day? Everyone dresses up in colonial costumes, even the teachers, and we bring old-style food to school. I think I'll bring Devonshire tea this year."

I could not help thinking how much younger these girls seemed than my friends back home, excited about playing dress-ups. But I tried to join in. "I have a costume," I said, "and my father is going to make pikelets."

One of the girls said, rudely, "How funny - your father cooks?"

Ann said, sounding cross, "Be quiet, Gweneth. You know Caitlin doesn't have a mother."

Gweneth put her hand over her mouth. "Sorry."

I stared at Ann. "How do you know about my mother?"

Ann tossed one of her long braids over her shoulder. "Miss Shock always tells us about the new girls so that we'll be kind to them."

"Are you being kind to me because I don't have a mother?"

"Of course not. You'll be very popular, once everyone gets to know you. What House are you in? The different Houses compete against each other for points in sports and academics."

"I think I'm in Blaxland House," I said.

Ann smiled. "That's my House, too."

Gweneth said, "You have to make your own apron in domestic science, Caitlin."

"Caitlin knows about that," Ann said, with a proprietary air. "Hush, Miss Shock is speaking."

"The girls are knitting sweaters for themselves," the domestic science teacher said, in my next class. "Can you knit, Caitlin?"

"No, ma'am," I replied.

"I am Mrs. Chatterton. You must learn to knit in this class."

Ann said, "I could show her, Mrs. Chatterton."

"That is very nice of you, Ann. You can choose a pattern from one of my books."

"Where do I buy the yarn?" I asked, starting to feel anxious.

Ann said, "You can buy wool at the shopping center in Emu Plains. I'll teach you to knit, if you will teach me how to do the Texas two-step when my knee is better."

~~~

"How did things go?" my father asked. "Did you make any friends at school?"

"I think I made one friend," I said, cautiously.

"Good." I could hear the relief in his voice, even over the phone. "How were the classes?"

"Okay. I am going to need help with history, and I have to learn to knit."

"Australian history? We'll get you a tutor. Enid can probably help with the knitting. I should be home around six o'clock tonight. Make sure you have something to eat, won't you?"

I put down the phone. Back in Dallas, I hardly ever came home to an empty house. My mother, or Doris the housekeeper, had always been there with milk and cookies or hot chocolate for me. This house seemed so empty and quiet. There was a television set in the living-room, but with only a few channels to watch; and all my father's videos were of cricket matches.

Sighing, I went to my bedroom to change out of my school uniform. I was combing my hair in the mirror when I noticed, behind me, a row of tiny black paw marks on the fireplace. They went along the mantle shelf as well. Could a squirrel have come down the chimney, or a possum? Did they have squirrels in Australia? I had heard of bandicoots, but they were little burrowing animals. I bent down and peered into the fireplace, but I could not see anything in the blackness.

I liked the idea of having a furry visitor, so long as I knew what it was. My father had said the wildlife was protected in New South Wales. Did that mean wild animals could come into the house? I was in the kitchen, making a peanut-butter sandwich and thinking about the strange little footprints, when Sebastian popped into the house through the cat door. No, the marks on the fireplace were not cat paws.

I gave Sebastian his food, and then I took my snack and my school books and went to sit on the back porch. French class had not been so bad, though the teacher spoke French with an Australian accent, and geography - well, geography was the same everywhere. But I would have to study hard to catch up in history. The other girls were working on projects about a historical figure, and fortunately Mr. Mackerel paired me with another student for that assignment.

From the porch, I could see large black birds - Currawongs - sitting in the gum trees next door. They were calling to each other and making the most awful noise. Sebastian started to meow, his green eyes shining with excitement. The noise of the birds grew louder and louder as an elderly woman came outside and set a tin plate of bread on a tree stump for the swooping birds.

She waved to me. "Hello, lovie."

I waved back, but I could feel tears prickling the backs of my eyes. The first day at school had been bearable, and my father was making plans to take me to the zoo in Sydney at the weekend. But, for some reason, the sight of the gray-haired lady in her garden made me feel so lonely that I gathered up my books and hurried back into the house. I did not know how I was going to get through the rest of the afternoon, let alone the rest of my life, without my mother. I was about to have what my mother called "a little cry."

CHAPTER 6

To: "Dr. Tim Robbins" <timrob@onramp.net>

Subject: Family news

Aunt Natalie, Uncle Tim, Marybeth, Alicia, and Peter,

I thought I would e-mail you instead of calling, in case I start to cry. I don't want to do that because everything is really okay. I am just homesick for you, and America. I have been going to Tennyson College for about a week. The other girls are friendly and the teachers are nice, but I have to wear this awful brown uniform.

Dad is okay. We are getting along well. I haven't seen any Australian animals yet, but I think a possum came into the house one night. Dad put a piece of wire over the chimney to stop it, but in a way, I wish he hadn't.

Please e-mail me and let me know how you are. Dad has set me up on his computer. I will call soon, too. By the way, did you know he is getting married? I have met his fiancé. She has red hair.

I miss you all. Love,

Caitlin.

CHAPTER 7

History Day

"You look beautiful, Caitlin," Ann said. "Where did you get a lovely dress like that?"

I looked down at my long calico skirt. "From my father's antique store. He says it's not really old. It was made for a play or something."

"It looks just like a real colonial gown, with the high waist and everything." Ann took my hand. "Didn't I tell you this would be fun?"

I was enjoying myself. All the teachers were in costume. Even Miss Shock was wearing a long black gown. "I may look a little too Victorian for colonial times," she told us, when we were assembled in the refectory, "but, like you, I have done my best to get into the spirit of History Day."

There were no regular classes scheduled for the whole day. Every classroom had some kind of old-fashioned activity for us to try. Mr. Mackerel joked that we were going to play "two-up," which was a game of chance. He had actually brought along indoor bowls, showing us how to play with an air of good-natured superiority.

I put my plate of pikelets on the trestle-table alongside Ann's scones and Gweneth's apricot bread. Outside in the quadrangle, the physical education teacher had set up deck tennis and croquet. Ann could not run about, so Gweneth and I spent most of the day sitting on the lawn with her, while other girls laughed and argued over the croquet mallets.

"We are supposed to be colonial ladies," Ann said. "They didn't do much except embroider and write letters. Their convict-servants did all the work."

"If I had been alive then," Gweneth said, gloomily, "I probably would have been a convict."

"I would have been a lady," Ann said.

"I think I would have been a governess," I said. "You know, it is funny the way America was founded on freedom and Australia was founded by convicts."

"You had bond servants in America," Gweneth said, biting into a coconut macaroon. "That's really what the convicts were - bond servants."

"You had slaves in America, too," Ann added. "Australia never had slaves."

"Not everyone in America owned slaves," I began.

"Not all convicts had a dreadful life. Some of them were---" Ann stumbled over the word, "rehabilitated."

I felt so comfortable with my new friends, I had spoken without thinking. Of course they would not want me to criticize anything about Australia. "I know that, Ann."

Ann reached over and patted my hand. "Let's talk about something else. Your pikelets are very good."

"You haven't had a piece of Miss Shock's meringue dessert, Caitlin," Gweneth said. "It is yummy."

As soon as I arrived home from school, I took off my back-pack and tossed it on the floor. I was too tired to change my clothes and so, still wearing my colonial costume, I unlocked the kitchen door and called to Sebastian. But there was no sign of the little cat, so I called again, "Sebastian!" When he did not appear, I gathered up my long skirt and went down to the back fence to open the old wooden gate.

"Are you looking for someone?"

I turned around, startled. A young man was standing under the willow trees, watching me. He was dressed in riding clothes and he was carrying what looked like an artist's sketch book. "Sebastian is our cat," I said, breathlessly. "Have you seen him?"

"Not that I know of. What does he look like?"

"He is small and black," I said.

The boy came closer. He was taller than I was, and very fair. He was wearing jodhpurs and a white shirt with a fashionably narrow collar, and beautiful leather boots. He looked so "preppy" that I guessed he was one of the Brebner boys Ann and Gweneth talked about. "Are you new here?" he asked.

It crossed my mind that I should not be talking to this young stranger, but I was just outside my own gate. "I've been here for a couple of weeks." I pointed to the cottage on the hill. "I live there with my father."

"In the superintendent's house? May I ask your name?"

"Caitlin. Caitlin Pritchard."

"I am Ainsley Allen." He said his name as though I should know him, the way good-looking boys sometimes did.

"How do you do?" I said, copying Enid Durham.

"Were you sent out?" the boy asked.

"Sent?" I was puzzled. "No, I wanted to come here."

"Excuse my saying so, but are you foreign?"

"I am from Texas," I told him.

"Where is that?"

I could not help smiling. "You don't know where

Texas is? Where do you go to school?"

"I have a private tutor," Ainsley said.

"You are home schooled?"

"Yes, I am educated at home."

"Texas is in America," I told him.

"The United States of America?" the boy asked.

What other America was there? "I lived in Boston as well as in Texas," I said.

"I have read all about Boston and the colonials' war against King George. The Americans were very brave."

We stood looking at one another for a moment. "I see you like to draw," I said.

Ainsley tucked his sketch book under his arm. "These are just some sketches I have been doing in my spare time."

I detected a different accent, too. "Are you English?"

"My father came here from London a long time ago. He was granted this land by Governor Macquarie. Before that, we lived in Parramatta."

Suddenly, my legs began to tremble and I had to sit down on the grass, "Oh, dear."

"Are you ill?" Ainsley asked, looking concerned.

I put my hand on my forehead. I felt cold, not hot. "I think I must have been outside too long."

"Perhaps you have a touch of the sun. I will fetch some water from the creek."

"The creek isn't running," I said. "Anyway, my father says the water isn't fit to drink."

"It looks quite clear," Ainsley said. "The duckbills play further upstream." I watched him hurry to the creek and come back with a metal flask. "You should wear a hat outdoors, Miss Pritchard."

"Everyone tells me that." I took a sip of the cool water in the flask and it tasted fine. I leaned back against the fence, feeling better. "What are duckbills?"

"Have you not seen one?" Ainsley's voice was excited. "They are the strangest creatures. They look like a mole, but they have the bill and feet of a duck." He was suddenly distracted. "What is that on your wrist?"

"My watch? It is an American one."

"I have never seen a watch like that."

Other girls at Tennyson College had digital watches. I wondered if Ainsley had been kept isolated from other people. "Where did you say you lived?"

He pointed towards the shopping center. "In the homestead. You cannot see it from here. It is just over that rise."

For some reason, the tips of my fingers began to tingle. "I am sorry, but I think I had better go inside."

"Will I see you tomorrow?" Ainsley asked.

If Ainsley Allen were home schooled, I guessed he was lonelier than I was. "My father is taking me into Sydney tomorrow."

"The day after that is the Sabbath," Ainsley said. "What about on Monday? Would you be able to meet me on Monday?"

"I usually have homework to do in the afternoon," I said.

"Will you try to come, all the same? I would very much like to talk with you again."

I stood up unsteadily. "If I do, will you show me some of your drawings?"

Politely, Ainsley put out his hand to help me. "I might. May I escort you to your door?"

I smiled. "You don't have to do that. I'm all right."

I opened the gate to my father's backyard. The noisy Currawongs were congregating next door, waiting for the neighbor to feed them, as usual. Just then, Sebastian appeared from around the side of the house, meowing for attention. I bent to pick him up, almost tripping on my long skirt. I looked back over my shoulder to the vacant lot, expecting to wave good-bye to my new friend. But the boy had disappeared amongst the willow trees. I suddenly realized that he had not said anything about the quaint way I was dressed. I supposed he was too polite to mention my clothes.

CHAPTER 8

Taronga Zoo

On Saturday, as he had promised, my father took me on an excursion to the city. We woke up early, drove to Emu Plains railway station and took the train into Sydney. On the wharf, we caught the ferry across the gorgeous harbor to Taronga Zoo.

I had expected Enid Durham to come with us, but my father said, "Enid is going to take care of the shop for me."

"I wouldn't have minded if she had come with us," I said, politely.

"Maybe she can come next time."

The first thing I wanted to see at the zoo was a koala. The little marsupials were as beautiful and as cuddly as they looked on television, but very sleepy. After that, I led my father to the platypus enclosure. "Is there another name for a platypus?" I asked, thinking about Ainsley.

"People used to call them duckbills." Standing at the exhibit, my father said, "I never liked zoos, but we have taken so much of their habitat, the zoo is the only place some of these animals are going to survive. Are you hungry? We could go back on the ferry and have lunch in the Rocks District. It is a historical part of Sydney."

"That sounds great."

On the train going home, I felt like a little girl, tired after a wonderful day out with my father. I could not help thinking about all the other outings we had missed in the past. My father was so easy to be with that I finally asked him the question, "Why did you and Mom get divorced?"

He turned his head. "Didn't your mother tell you?"

"She used to say your marriage came to its logical conclusion, but I am not sure what she meant."

"Personally, I think it had something to do with geography."

"Geography?"

"I wanted to live in Australia and your mother wanted to be in Texas."

~ ~ ~

"You went to the zoo with your father?" Gweneth grimaced. "I was ten years old the last time I went to the zoo."

"Caitlin hadn't been to Taronga before," Ann said, giving Gweneth a poke in the ribs. "Don't be rude."

I said, defensively, "I love animals."

"So do I," Ann said. It was the lunch hour and we were sitting under a tree behind the science building. "Tell us more about your new boy-friend, Caitlin."

I felt my face getting warm. "Ainsley isn't my boy-friend. He is just a friend."

"Ainsley," Gweneth repeated. "That is a funny name."

Ann said, seriously, "You know his father couldn't have been given land by Governor Macquarie, don't you?"

I stared at Ann. "Why not?"

"Because," Ann said, as though repeating a lesson, "Governor Macquarie left Australia almost two hundred years ago."

My heart started to pound. "Are you sure?"

"You can look it up for yourself in the history books. Governor Macquarie came to Australia in 1809, and he left in 1822."

"Who is the governor of Australia now?"

"Australia has a governor-general, but his name isn't Macquarie, and he doesn't give out land to people. I think your friend is telling stories."

"He is having you on because you're an American," Gweneth said. "Next, he'll be telling you that we use kangaroos for bus conductors."

I remembered the way Ainsley had stared at my digital watch. Had he really been kidding me? Ann said, "Or he might be a bit soft in the head."

"Not the full two-bob," Gweneth added.

I shook my head. "Ainsley isn't like that. He seems very bright."

Ann and Gweneth looked at one another and giggled. "You sound like you are smitten by an Aussie hunk."

I tried to smile. "I haven't told my father about him yet."

Ann said, "Maybe you shouldn't. Fathers are funny about boys. My father wouldn't let me talk to one boy I know because he saw him wearing a red shirt."

Gweneth said, "If it were me, I would want to know if Ainsley has been in the psychiatric ward."

"Does Ainsley go to Brebner?" Ann asked.

"No," I said, "he is home schooled."

"I'll bet he's doing correspondence lessons because he's a mental case," Gweneth insisted.

"He is not a mental case. He is just old-fashioned."

"He must be old-fashioned," Ann said, giving her infectious smile, "if his father got his land from Governor Macquarie. Does he have a girl-friend?"

"I don't know," I began.

"Does he have a car?"

"I think Ainsley has a horse."

"If he has a horse," Ann said, "he probably lives on acreage. His father might be a doctor at the hospital. Are you coming to our dance, Caitlin?"

Gweneth answered for me, teasing, "Not if Ainsley won't be there."

~ ~ ~

Despite my friends' doubts, I was looking forward to seeing Ainsley again. He was not like any of the boys I had known back home. To begin with, he did not chew gum, or put his baseball cap on back to front, or wear his shirt hanging out of his trousers. And he did not use gross language or ask rude questions like, "Are you still a virgin?"

So, why had I not told my father about this boy who looked "preppy" and was so well-mannered? I supposed I wanted to keep Ainsley to myself a little longer. Anyway, I knew he might not even show up again. Why would such a good-looking boy bother with me? I had been so "uncool", falling down at his feet like that. My faced burned, remembering.

"Good-afternoon, Miss Pritchard."

Ainsley was standing beside the creek dressed in riding clothes, but he was wearing a jacket this time. He had a portable easel set up on the grass and a little folding chair. "Would you care to sit down?"

I smiled. "What are you drawing?"

"I am sketching the cottage where you live," he replied.

"Can I see it?" I asked.

Ainsley stepped aside so that I could look at the sketch on the easel. My mother had taken me to exhibitions at the Dallas Museum of Art and the Kimball Art Museum. I was prepared to like Ainsley's sketch no matter how mediocre it was; but I was startled at the way, with a few lines on the paper, he captured the charm of the little house on the hill. He had added several gum trees sheltering the roof, which were not actually there, but it was a beautiful drawing of my father's cottage.

"Do you like it?" he asked.

I looked up. "I think it is wonderful. Where did you learn to draw like this?"

Ainsley shrugged. "One of my teachers showed me a few techniques."

"You are very talented. Have you thought about

going to art school? You could be an illustrator or something."

"I would never be allowed to study art abroad."

"I didn't mean abroad." I stopped. "I am sorry. I don't know anything about schools in Australia. I didn't mean to be nosy."

He was smiling. "There is no need to apologize. I am pleased you like my drawing."

"I wish my mother were here to see it. She knew a lot about art."

"Your mother passed away?" Ainsley asked.

"Last year," I replied.

"My mother died when I was a child."

"But you have your father?"

Ainsley reached over my shoulder and signed his name on the left-hand corner of the sketch. "My father has no patience with anything that I am interested in."

Standing so close to him, I found myself almost mesmerized by Ainsley's finely sculptured profile, more a work of art than even his sketch. The sun was beating down on my head and all I could see was his face and the white of his shirt. "What are you going to do with the drawing of the cottage?" I asked, diffidently. "I would love to have it."

Ainsley immediately took the sketch from the easel, rolled it up, and handed it to me with a flourish. "I would be grateful if you would not show it to anyone else."

"Why not? Aren't you proud of your work?"

"I suppose I am, but my father thinks I waste my time drawing. He is away from home, which is the reason I am able to come here this afternoon."

"Where has your father gone?"

"To Sydney Town. He spends a lot of time there."

"Do you ever go with him?" I asked.

"I have been to Sydney Town," Ainsley said, shortly.

"Do you have any other friends, beside your teacher, I mean?"

"I am not permitted to fraternize with the lower classes. I was brought up a gentleman. May I ask you something?"

I was clutching the sketch. My palms felt moist. "Of course."

"Are you a blue-stocking?" Ainsley asked.

"What is that?"

"A lady who is learned - literary. I thought that might be the reason you wear men's clothes."

Of course, he was talking about the designer shirt and jeans I was wearing. "This is how girls dress where I come from."

"In Texas? I must say I like it, Miss Pritchard."

I dropped a curtsy, the way I had learned in dance class. "Please call me Caitlin."

CHAPTER 9

Dancing

Enid Durham insisted on helping me choose a dress to wear to the school dance. In my bedroom, I let her look through my wardrobe, though I did not really need or want her opinion.

"Any of these would be perfectly suitable," Enid said. "What about this one?" She held up a "granny-print" skirt with a matching sweater. The outfit was one of my favorites.

"If you think so," I said, without enthusiasm.

"You do want to go to the dance, don't you?" Enid asked.

"I suppose I do."

"You know it is not compulsory?"

"Miss Shock says all the students should be there."

"But Miss Shock realizes you are still in mourning for your mother, doesn't she?"

"Of course she does." I turned away from Enid and began tidying my dressing-table. She should have known it was easier to go to the silly dance than make a fuss about it with the headmistress.

My father came to the door. "Are you girls ready?"

Enid began putting the clothes back in the wardrobe. "I don't know about Caitlin, but I'm starving."

"Thanks for your help, Enid," I said.

Enid frowned. "I don't think I was much help."

My father had made reservations for us to have dinner at a country restaurant in the lower Blue Mountains. Afterwards, we drove up to Mt. Riverview so that I could see the view of the valley at night.

"Real estate agents here talk about the twinkling city lights," my father said, getting out of the car, "and they are right."

I climbed out of the car. Spread below, like jewels on a velvet carpet, were the lights of Emu Plains and Penrith and, on the distant horizon, the city lights of Sydney. "It looks like fairyland."

"I always have trouble picking out our house," my father said. "That bright patch is the prison farm, which isn't far from where we live."

For some reason, I thought about Ainsley. Did he live at the prison farm? Perhaps his father was the warden. That would explain his isolation. "I didn't know there was a prison in Emu Plains."

"It is a low security place for young fellows who

have stolen a car - that sort of thing. Had enough?"

Enid was sitting in the front passenger's seat, waiting for us. "How about coming to my house for coffee?" she asked.

My father looked at me. "Okay?"

"Okay," I agreed.

Enid and my father sat by the fire drinking coffee while I wandered around Enid's living-room, feeling self-conscious. Finally, I asked, "Is it all right if I have a look at the art gallery?"

"Of course," Enid said. "The light switch is just inside the door, on the left."

I opened the adjoining door and turned on the lights, illuminating the small gallery. Enid called after me, "I have some new watercolors you might be interested in, Caitlin. They are on the south wall."

"Thank you," I called back.

Enid had dozens of oil paintings and watercolors arranged around the room - paintings hanging one above the other - and boxes of prints standing against the walls. There were no windows or furniture except a few chairs, but I liked the emptiness of the space. On the far wall, I found the paintings that Enid spoke about. One of them drew my eye straight away. It was a bush scene with a winding river in the background displayed behind glass in a delicate gold frame. It was so real, I could have stepped into it, and the artist had captured that peculiar blue light that glowed from the Australian forest.

Fascinated, I leaned forward to look at the artist's signature in the corner. The name and the signature were familiar: "Ainsley Allen."

"Enid!"

"What is it? Is something wrong?"

"No, not really," I said, quickly, going to the door. "I just wanted to ask you something about one of your paintings."

Enid came into the gallery. "What did you want to know?"

I led her over to the little watercolor. "Where did you get this?"

"Those three paintings came from a deceased estate in Leura, which is a town further up the mountains."

"A deceased estate?"

"You know - an estate sale. The paintings are quite valuable, but they are not mine. I am handling them for the new owner, acting as his agent."

"Why are they so valuable?" I hoped my voice

sounded normal.

"Because they were painted by nineteenth century Australian artists."

"Nineteenth century?"

"The Ainsley Allen is probably the most sought after. There has already been a lot of interest in this painting - so much so, I am thinking of sending it to Sydney for auction." Enid put out her hand and touched the frame. "It is exquisite, isn't it?"

I tried to keep my eyes focused on the painting. "How much do you think it is worth?"

"I expect it will fetch a high price - thousands of dollars, probably. There is a strong market for anything to do with colonial Australia these days, especially a work of such quality."

"Are you sure this one was painted that long ago?"

"Quite sure. Some of Allen's watercolors are hanging in galleries in Sydney. He is better known for his pen-and-ink sketches. His collection of Australian animals is just wonderful. He left a relatively small body of work, so we think he died young."

"Do you have any of his sketches?"

"I could get you a print, if you want one."

I had to ask, "Do you know if he has any---any descendants who are artists?"

"Not that I know of. Of course, we don't know much about him, except that he lived in the colony and probably died in the 1820's. Talent like that sometimes does run in families."

Well, I said to myself, this artist cannot be "my" Ainsley Allen, not if he died in the 1820's. But, to my untrained eye, the signature on the painting on Enid's wall and the sketch in my closet looked exactly the same.

"When in doubt, wash," my mother used to say. Of course, she had been talking about our cat, but the advice was still sound. At home, I filled the green bathtub with hot water, climbed in, and soaked myself until the water was nearly cold. I spent the rest of the evening pouring over history books, reading everything I could find about colonial Australia. I learned very little about Emu Plains, except that it had been declared a township by Governor Macquarie. I found nothing in the text about colonial artists.

As I was reading, the poet Robert Browning's words about a "hopeful past" kept running through my head. I could not help wondering whether Ainsley's past had been hopeful; and what about the present-day? Why was he pretending to be something that he was not?

~~~

I liked the boys from Brebner Academy that I met

at the school dance. They were nicely dressed and they danced all the dances. None of them hung about the door of the refectory or tried to sneak outside for a cigarette. Of course, they were closely chaperoned by Miss Shock and the other teachers.

"They have to behave themselves at our dances," Gweneth said, "otherwise they get into trouble with their headmaster on Monday."

Though Ann could not dance, there was always a Brebner boy sitting with her while everyone else was out on the floor. An older boy with dark curly hair came over to me. "May I have this dance? My name is Barry Egan-Smith."

I stood up. Barry was so tall that I had to crane my neck to see his face. "Pleased to meet you," I said, taking his hand. "I am Caitlin."

"I went to Disney World with my father last year," he said, when he realized I was an American. "It is an incredible place."

"Is it? I've been to Disneyland," I said. "That's the one in California."

Out on the dance floor, Barry asked, "What does your father do?"

"He is an antique dealer."

"Is he American, too?"

"No," I said, "he is an Australian."

"My father is a bigwig in Canberra, and my mother is a stockbroker," Barry said. "They are divorced now."

"My mother was a real estate broker," I offered.

"Was?"

"She was killed in a car accident last year."

"That must have been tough." Barry's voice was genuinely sympathetic.

"Yes," I said, "it was."

"One of my friends is having a party next Saturday night. Would you like to come with me?"

"Will other Tennyson girls be going?" I asked.

"I think so. Can I give you a ring - call you, I mean?"

I smiled. "If you like."

"You have won yourself a heart," Ann said, when the band was taking a break. "Barry Egan-Smith is a twelfth grader and a prefect."

"What is a prefect?" I asked.

"An older student who stands in for the teachers. We used to have them at Tennyson. Barry is on the rowing team. He'll probably invite you to watch him race."

"He wants me to go to a party next week."

Ann said, "Don't go to any of their parties, Caitlin. The boys are different at private parties. They smoke and drink and do all kinds of things you don't want to know about."

"Barry seems nice." But I could not help feeling disappointed. It was only later that I wondered if Ann might be jealous that she had not been invited to the party as well.

CHAPTER 10

Finding Ainsley

"Ainsley Allen! Ainsley Allen!"

My eyes flew open. I was in my room, in my bed. It was my voice that had been saying Ainsley's name over and over in a dream, calling him, but getting no answer.

I sat up and gathered the comforter around me. As my father had warned me, it could be cold in the house at night without central heating. I could hear the mantle clock in the living-room striking the hour: three in the morning, the worst time to be awake. Twelve o'clock was not so bad, or even two, but nobody else was ever awake at three o'clock.

When the chiming stopped, I could hear water dripping down the guttering into the iron tank outside my window. It must have rained through the night. I stretched out my feet, grateful for Sebastian's warm, soft body on the bed. Staring into the darkness, I decided that I needed to know the reason Ainsley was telling lies, pretending to be an artist, even lying about his name. Well, I could not be sure about that. Enid Durham did not know everything. Ainsley might be descended from an Australian painter with the same name. He said his family had come to New South Wales a long time ago.

I smoothed my pillow and lay back under the covers. "Sebastian," I told the cat, "we need to find out who Ainsley really is, and where he lives."

Sebastian climbed up to my neck and licked my face with his rough little tongue.

~ ~ ~

On Saturday afternoon, while my father was at his antique store, I put on my sneakers and went out to the vacant lot to explore. Before I left the house, I made sure Sebastian was locked inside so that he could not follow me and get lost.

The winding creek bed was dry, despite rain the night before. Once I was on the eastern embankment, I climbed the small hill and stood on top of the rise. I expected to see at least one house, but the land was fenced with barbed wire and ran into a concrete parking lot for the shopping center. Most of the brush had been cleared away, except for an old eucalyptus tree with its roots embedded in the asphalt.

Yet Ainsley had pointed in this direction, telling me that he lived on the other side of the creek. Was that a lie, too? The possums were about the only creatures that could live here. Puzzled, I turned and went back down the embankment. My father had said there was a graveyard near his house. Maybe some of the Allen family were buried there.

Sure enough, as I walked further downstream, I could see a small cemetery silhouetted on the horizon. As I drew closer, I realized that the graves were protected by a rusty iron fence, but weeds had taken over the plots. From somewhere in the distance, I heard the sound of children playing, and shouting coming from what was probably a football game. Watching out for snakes, I knelt in the long grass to look at the half-dozen headstones wedged into the ground. Though I ran my fingers over the words, I could not make out any of the inscriptions. The graves had stood in the weather too long.

I looked back over my shoulder. I spied the roof of my father's house and the spire of the little chapel at Tennyson College. To the west, the wooded escarpment of the Blue Mountains rose up to the sky. This must have been a beautiful spot one hundred years ago. It was still beautiful, in spite of roads and drains and electric-light poles. But there were no answers to any of my questions about Ainsley.

"Dad---."

My father was taking a casserole dish out of the oven while I finished setting the table for dinner. "Dad," I repeated, "do you know the name of the people who owned this land in the old days?"

He put the hot dish down on the table and took off the oven mitts. "I know the name of the people I bought the house from."

I tried to keep my voice light. "But they weren't the first owners?"

"No, the cottage was probably built in the early 1800's."

"Who owned it when it was first built?"

"No one knows for sure. When I was buying the place, the lawyer searching the title couldn't find any records going back further than about 1880."

"What about the woman next door? Would she know anything about the families who lived here?"

"Maud is not that old," my father said. "Why are you asking about the house? Do you have a project for school?"

"Something like that," I said. "Was your house really built by convicts?"

"So I was told by the builder who worked on it for me."

"How did he know?"

"He could tell by the materials they had used and the way the house was constructed. Most of the workmen in the early days were convicts."

"There was a house on the other side of the creek, wasn't there?" I persisted.

My father reached for the tomato sauce. He put tomato sauce on almost everything. "Until they built the new supermarket."

"What was it like?"

"The old homestead? It was quite a large house, though it was only one room wide. I thought it was a pity they didn't try harder to rescue it, but a tree doctor was able to save the gum tree."

"Would there be any way to find out who built the homestead?" I asked.

"There's a little museum in Emu Plains at the old inn," my father said. "You might be able to look through their records, if it is for school. But be warned. I've heard there is a ghost who haunts the place. Someone apparently saw a young girl in an old-fashioned bonnet in one of the rooms, sitting on the end of the bed. But when the woman turned right around to look at her, she was gone."

I drew in my breath. "Do you believe in ghosts?"

"I believe in the spirit world. You have to, if you believe in life after death."

"Do you think spirits come back to haunt people?"

"I don't know," my father said. "Some of the

furniture in my shop has a spooky aura about it, as though it has absorbed trauma over the years."

"When could I go there?" I asked.

"To the museum? It is probably open at the weekend, but let me know if you plan to wander about the countryside, won't you?"

"I will tell you when I am going to the museum," I promised.

~ ~ ~

At four o'clock in the afternoon, I came home from school, changed into my jeans, and immediately went to try to find Ainsley. I unlatched the gate, but I could not see him anywhere along the creek. I felt a pang of disappointment. All my dreaming and thinking about him and my determination to find him had been a waste of time. But, as I walked through the weeping willows, I caught a glimpse of a white shirt amongst the branches. Ainsley was leaning against the trunk of a tree with his head bowed.

"Ainsley!" I saw him brush his hand across his eyes and I wondered if he had been crying. "Is something wrong?"

He looked up. "I am just feeling sorry for myself."

I reached into my pocket. "I have brought you some American candy."

Ainsley tried to smile. "Thank you. That is very kind of you, Caitlin."

I watched him carefully unwrap a piece of chocolate, thinking how handsome he was, and very blond, for a boy. "Are you sure you are all right?"

"I had a falling out with my father, that is all." Then, in a rush, Ainsley said, "He thinks I should be attending to my studies and have manly interests like riding and shooting. He says drawing is an occupation for young ladies."

"Jackson Pollock was masculine enough," I said.

"Who is Jackson Pollock?"

"You've never heard of Pollock, the American painter?"

"No," Ainsley said. "In the event, my father took all my drawings and put them in the fire."

I was horrified. "All of them?"

"Except the ones I had hidden under the bed."

"What are you going to do?"

"Wait until he goes to Sydney Town, then do some more," Ainsley said.

"Won't that be disobeying him?" I asked.

"I cannot live without my work."

"Could you talk to him about it?"

"Talking only makes problems worse," Ainsley said.

"Who told you that?" I said. "Talking can help solve problems."

"The contention with my father is my drawing. No amount of talking will change that."

"What about your teacher? Could he help you?"

"My teacher would not dare contradict my father," Ainsley said. "He needs his position."

I thought about the painting hanging in Enid's gallery. "But there have been other artists in your family, haven't there?"

"My father was a good forger, which is art of a kind, I suppose."

"Your father was a forger?" I could not keep the surprise out of my voice.

"He was given a pardon by the governor," Ainsley said, "but the stigma of having been a convict is still with him."

"If he was pardoned---" I began.

"That was only a formality. The governor gave him land at Parramatta to make a new start."

"Where do you live now?"

"I live here," Ainsley said. "This is part of our

farm."

"This is government land," I said.

"Some of the land at Emu Island is owned by government, but not this section."

"Where is your house?"

"On the other side of the creek."

I had to ask, "Ainsley, are you seeing a psychiatrist?"

"What is a psychiatrist?"

I was starting to feel annoyed with him. "You must know what a psychiatrist is - a doctor who treats people who are mentally ill."

He smiled suddenly. "Do you think I am a lunatic?"

"Well," I said, choosing my words carefully, "one of us is imagining things. I've had a lot of changes lately, with my mother dying and everything, but I don't think I am crazy. If you did live in the old homestead, it must have been a long time ago. I have been across the creek. There is no house there now."

"Never mind that," Ainsley said, suddenly sounding cheerful again. "Come with me. I want to show you something."

CHAPTER 11

Bush Walking

"What is the matter?" Ainsley asked, when I hesitated to follow him. "Do you not trust me?"

It was such an outdated thing to say, like something from a 1950's movie. "Of course I do," I said. "It is only that I need to be home before my father."

"Don't worry. We will be home in time for tea."

"Where are we going?" I asked.

"Into the foothills of the Blue Mountains," Ainsley announced.

"Before we go, I need to ask you something. Do you have a girl-friend?"

He looked puzzled. "A girl-friend?"

"Someone you like very much, that you are close to," I said.

"Do you want to be my girl-friend?"

I was touched by his lack of sophistication. "Perhaps we should wait till we know each other a little better."

"If you wish," he agreed. "Are you ready to go?"

Ainsley took my hand and suddenly I was running with him over the soft grass that grew alongside the creek. I felt as though my feet barely touched the ground. We were traveling upstream, climbing into the hills as we followed the path of the creek, crossing bracken and ferns, gullies and rock pools. When we finally stopped and turned to look back, I could see the treetops below and the wattle ablaze with yellow flowers like clusters of sunshine amongst the gum trees. Yet I was not even out of breath.

"Can you see the black cockatoos?" Ainsley pointed to a clump of low trees ahead of us. I heard the birds screeching before I saw the large black parrots. "And through there," he said, "is a pheasant with feathers shaped like a lyre. I am going to paint it one day."

"Ainsley, that is a lyre bird."

"You know what it is?"

"I have seen pictures in the National Geographic - a magazine," I added, automatically, knowing he would not understand.

"Look down into the stream," Ainsley said.

I looked down into the water eddying over the stones at my feet. The water was so clear, I could see the sand at the bottom. I noticed a movement in the creek and at first I thought it was a large fish. I looked again and saw the furry body and bill of a platypus, and then I spotted another one playing on the surface and diving in the water. I could not help thinking about Mr. Mackerel's Australian history class: "Water moles are to be found in abundance in every stream and lake", a traveler in New South Wales had written in the 1820's.

I took a step forward, but Ainsley held me back. "They are very shy. If they know we are here, they will disappear. They have their nest in the bank."

"Do you know how incredible this is - platypus so close to the city? I thought they were only in zoos."

"Duckbills are everywhere in the creek," Ainsley answered. "Let's go further into the bush. There is something else I want to show you."

We went hand in hand, higher into the hills. "Now," Ainsley said, "look up."

I lifted my eyes until I could see two koalas resting sleepily in the gum trees overhead. One of them had a baby koala on her back. "They eat the leaves of the eucalyptus trees," Ainsley said. "I think it makes them sleepy."

I stood very still, staring up at the small wonders in the branches. "Are you having a good time, Caitlin?" Ainsley asked.

"You chose the thing I most wanted to see - koalas living in the wild," I said. "Now all I need is a kangaroo hopping past."

"There are hundreds of kangaroos in the bush. You will see one soon enough."

We climbed on to an outcrop of rock and sat looking down on the plains and the winding Nepean River. I could not see any buildings or poles, nothing except the bush and a few clearings in the distance. "You have been so nice to me," I said. "Is there anything I can do for you?"

"Since you asked me," Ainsley said, "I would give anything to have one of those watches."

"A digital watch? Do you want an American one?"

"Yes, please."

"I will get my Aunt Natalie to send you one from Boston. You are allowed to have modern things, aren't you?"

"Of course I am. Why do you ask me that?"

"I just wondered."

Ainsley reached into his coat pocket. "I brought you a poke of sugar-candy shipped from China."

"From China?" I took the little brown packet from him. "How exotic. I tell you what---." On an impulse, I unfastened my wrist-watch. "You can have this now. I will get another one from my aunt."

Ainsley accepted my gift graciously and put the watch on his wrist. I remembered my mother telling me that no one could be happy all the time, that you had moments in your life when you were happy. Well, this was one of those moments. I also understood something else. You could be happy no matter where you were, so long as you were with the right person.

Ainsley took a little notebook out of his pocket. "What are you doing?" I asked, curiously.

"I am sketching you. Please turn your head to the left."

I giggled, but I obediently turned my head.

"We are never going to die," Ainsley said.

"How do you figure that?" I asked.

"I will never be forgotten because I am the artist, and you - because you are the subject of my drawing."

Impulsively, I leaned over and kissed Ainsley on the cheek. I saw him color faintly, but he smiled and held out the sketch. "Do you like it?"

"I don't think I am as pretty as that, but I like it very much. May I have it?"

Ainsley shook his head. "I am keeping this one. I may paint your portrait one day, when I have the skills."

"You said your father doesn't want you to paint."

I saw a shadow pass over his face. We had both been so light-hearted as we climbed into the hills together. Incredibly, I had even forgotten about my mother for a little while. As abruptly as he had begun our adventure, Ainsley ended it. "Time to go," he said, closing the notebook, "if we want to get home before dark."

He stood up and offered me his hand.

~~~

"Where have you been, Caitlin?" My father sounded annoyed. "I came home early and I was beginning to think you had been kidnapped."

I was still feeling exhilarated after my excursion with Ainsley. "I am sorry, Dad. I guess I lost track of the time."

"Young lady, I asked you where you have been."

My father had never yelled at me before, but I knew he was worried, rather than really angry. "I just went for a walk in the bush."

"I thought you were going to tell me before you went traipsing about the place," he reminded me.

"I am sorry," I repeated.

He was calming down. "Well, never mind. You

are home now. Have you finished your homework?"

"Not yet."

"Go and get cleaned up and we will have dinner, then you can do the rest of your homework."

I went to wash my hands and comb my hair. From the bathroom across the hallway, I could hear my father talking on the phone to Enid, telling her the story.

CHAPTER 12

Failing French

At the door of the classroom, all my books went tumbling out of my arms on to the floor. "Why don't you have lockers at this school?" I said, irritably.

Ann Engels came up behind me. "You will get a locker when you're a senior," she said, helping me to retrieve my books.

"If I make it that far."

"What's the matter?" Ann asked. "Did you get up on the wrong side of the bed this morning?"

"I haven't studied for Mrs. Flynn's test," I said.

"Miss Flynn," Ann corrected me, as we went to our desks. "It will be a piece of cake. Did you see Ainsley yesterday?"

"For a while," I said. "That is why I didn't study."

"Does he have a steady girl-friend?"

"He didn't know what I was talking about," I said.

Ann frowned. "How old is this person?"

"About the same age as us," I said.

"Are you getting tired of him?"

"Of course not. Ainsley isn't the same as other boys. He is like Shelley."

"Shelley?" Ann asked.

"You know," I said, embarrassed, "the British poet. At least, he is the way I imagine Shelley would have been. He is an artist, and a bit unconventional."

Miss Flynn was taking attendance at the front of the class. "Ann and Caitlin, no talking, please."

"I gave him my watch," I blurted out.

Ann was staring at me. "Why did you do that?"

"Because I felt sorry for him."

"Does your father know?"

"It is my watch," I said. "I can do whatever I like with it."

"Ann Engels and Caitlin Pritchard," the teacher said, "if I hear another word from you two, you will both be in detention this afternoon."

"Yes, Miss Flynn," Ann said. She whispered to me, "We'll talk about it at lunch time."

Ann and I sat together in the refectory while Gweneth glared at us from another table. "Gweneth is a chatterbox," Ann said. "It is better not to say too much in front of her, unless you want the whole school to know your business."

I was looking at the large "C" that Miss Flynn had put on my French test. Ann said, "Don't worry. You'll do better next time."

"I hope so," I said, gloomily. "My father will be mad if he finds out."

"It won't be on your report card. I have been thinking you should ask Ainsley to give your watch back."

"I can't do that."

"Wasn't it a birthday present from your mother?" Ann asked.

"She gave me other things," I said. "It wasn't expensive."

"Why can't Ainsley get a watch of his own?"

"He doesn't know anything about the modern world."

"Why not?" Ann's voice was sharp.

"I don't know," I said. "It is strange, because his family seems to have plenty of money."

"He might be time-traveling," Ann said.

I put down my sandwich. "What do you mean?"

"Ainsley might have come from another time. I saw a movie about it. This writer went back in time and met a famous actress he saw in a photograph.

That would explain why Ainsley had never seen a digital watch."

When I was a little girl, my mother dropped a stack of saucepan lids on the kitchen floor and the sound clattered through my head. I had the same kind of sensation now, as though a thousand symbols were clanging together. Was Ainsley from the past? Was that what was happening? I said, weakly, "I never thought of that."

Ann smiled. "I'm not serious. My father says time travel is a lot of nonsense. I only said that because Ainsley is so behind the times. He doesn't go to school - like in the olden days."

"He showed me all the wildlife," I added.

"What wildlife?"

"Koalas and platypus."

"Where?" Ann asked.

"In Emu Plains," I replied.

"There aren't any koalas or platypus in Emu Plains." Ann giggled, nervously this time. "Did he show you any emus?"

"No, but he says there are kangaroos everywhere."

"There are not. Maybe he is a ghost. Lots of people have experiences with ghosts on television."

I was beginning to wonder if I had made Ainsley

up in my imagination. Was I so homesick that I would invent a boy to talk to after school? I said, firmly, "Ainsley isn't a ghost. He is real, just like us. I touched his hand. And he put my watch on his wrist like a regular person."

Gweneth came over to our table. "What are you two talking about?"

"Go away, Gweneth," Ann said. "This is a private conversation."

"Caitlin is my friend, too," Gweneth said.

"We are just talking about a problem I have," I said.

"Can I listen? I might be able to help you."

"It is a boy problem," Ann said. "You don't know anything about boys."

Gweneth pouted. "I know you're talking about the weird and wonderful Ainsley."

I stood up. "I am going to the common room for a while."

"I'll come with you," Gweneth said.

"Let her alone, Gweneth," Ann said.

"I am sorry," I said, "but I need to work on my French."

~~~

"Dad, is it all right if I go to the museum at Emu Plains this afternoon?" I asked. "I am still researching Australian history for that class project."

"Where did you say you were going?" my father asked, absently. It was early on Saturday morning, and he was getting ready to leave for his store.

"To the museum," I repeated.

"Is it open today?"

"It opens at eleven. I called - I mean, I rang them."

"Are you going to walk?" my father asked.

"How else can I get there?"

"You could ring me up when you are ready to come home."

"It's not far," I told him. "I can walk back."

"Are you sure? Don't accept a ride with anyone, will you?"

"No, Dad."

"Why aren't you going with one of your school friends?" my father wanted to know.

"Because no one else is doing this project," I said.

"What exactly are you looking for, dear?" the

volunteer at the museum asked.

The counter where I was standing looked as though it belonged in an old saloon. I had heard that this was a busy hotel in the olden days. "I am trying to find out about a family who used to live in Emu Plains," I said.

"How far back?" the woman asked.

"The early 1800's."

"Is this for your school work?"

"Yes, ma'am," I said.

"What is the name of the family?" she asked.

"Allen. One of them was a painter - Ainsley Allen. His family had a grant of land from Governor Macquarie."

The volunteer looked puzzled. "I have never heard that Ainsley Allen's family owned property in Emu Plains. If they did, it must have been for a very short time."

"You know about Ainsley Allen?" I asked.

"Of course. He is one of our national treasures."

"I was told the Allens still own land here."

"Really? I don't recall seeing the name in our journals." The woman reached behind her and took out a bundle of papers. "You can look through these, dear. If you don't find anything, you could try the church records. Have you been to the old cemetery?"

"Yes," I said, "but I couldn't read any of the names on the graves."

"We had a gentleman in here who was trying to decipher them. He is writing a book about local cemeteries. Do you want me to find his name for you?"

I took the bundle of papers from the counter. "Thank you, ma'am. Is it all right if I sit over there?"

"Yes, dear." The woman smiled. "I love the way Americans say 'ma'am.' You can have a look around the museum, if you like. I won't charge you."

"I've heard there is a ghost here," I said, cautiously.

"Quite right," she answered. "A couple of people have felt its presence in the front room, and one of our visitors actually came face to face with it."

"What kind of ghost was it?"

"It was in the form of a little girl."

I shivered. "Do you mean it wasn't really a little girl?"

"It might have been, but ghosts can take on other forms," the volunteer explained. "The trouble with ghosts is that they don't know they are ghosts. They think they are still in their own time. Some people say that spirits who haunt this world are trying to finish something left undone when they were alive."

I sat down at the table and opened the folder of notes. I already knew I was not going to find anything about the Allen family here. The ghost of the little girl might have some connection with them, but I was not going to research that.

CHAPTER 13

To: "Dr. Tim Robbins" <timrob@onramp.net>

Subject: Family news

Aunt Natalie, Uncle Tim, Marybeth, Alicia, and Peter,

I hope you are all well. I have kind of settled into Tennyson College. It is very different from an American school. Thank you for calling me last week. It was great to hear your voices. The weather here is good so far. I like it when it rains because we don't have sport. It is nice that Tiffany is happy with you, but I miss her a lot. Did I tell you Dad has a cat named Sebastian?

I have seen lots of Australian animals - platypus and koalas and birds. I am buying a camera so I can take pictures. Some of the candy is different here, so I will send you some. Let me know if there is anything else you want from Down Under.

Love,

Caitlin.

CHAPTER 14

A Visitor

"Caitlin, there is a young man here to see you!"

My heart skipped a beat. Ainsley must have come to visit me at home. I glanced at myself in the mirror. My hair was kind of tousled, but I looked presentable. But it was not Ainsley who was standing on the veranda with my father. "Barry!" I exclaimed.

"Hello, Caitlin." The boy I met at the school dance was smiling at me. He was dressed in jeans and a very white tee-shirt. Parked in front of our house was a sleek, black automobile.

I stammered, "How did you know where I lived?"

"You said your father sold antiques. I did a bit of detective work through the phone book. I hope you don't mind."

"No, of course not. Dad, this is Barry---."

"---Egan-Smith," Barry finished. "I met Caitlin at the school dance."

My father extended his hand. "You're a Brebner boy?"

"Yes, sir," Barry said, shaking hands with my father. "I've been going there since kindergarten."

"Do you live around here, Barry?" my father asked.

"I live in Penrith."

"Barry is on the school rowing team," I said.

"That's a great sport," my father said. "What year are you in at high school?"

"This is my final year," Barry said. "I'm hoping to go to uni' next year."

"Sydney University?"

"Yes, sir."

"What course?" my father asked.

"Medicine," Barry replied.

My father was cross-examining Barry as though he were courting me. "Do you want to come into the house, Barry?" I interrupted them.

"It's all right," Barry said. "I just wanted to come by and say hello."

"Well," Dad said, "I will leave you two to talk. I have work to do." He opened the screen door. "Would you like a soft-drink, Barry?"

"No, thank you, sir," Barry said.

"That is a nice car," I said, when my father had gone into the house.

Barry leaned against the veranda railing. In his blue jeans, he looked more at ease than he had at the dance. "It belongs to my mother. I have a car of my own, but it is an old bomb."

"A bomb?"

He smiled. "A heap, you would probably call it. I am supposed to be getting a new car from my father when I matriculate."

"I didn't know you wanted to be a doctor."

"Actually," Barry said, "I want to be a pediatrician."

"Is it hard to get into medical school?" I asked.

"It is hard to get into any course at Sydney Uni'. My teachers think I'll make it, but I am not that confident."

"Do you study a lot?"

"Most of the time, except when I'm rowing," Barry said. "Do you want to come and see me row on Saturday?"

I hesitated. "I would have to ask my dad."

"We always have a get-together afterwards, whether we win or not. It is at my house this time."

I remembered Ann's warning about Brebner boys and their parties. "What do you do at your parties?" I asked.

"We sit around and talk about the race, and dance and listen to music. Why?" Barry's voice had sharpened. "Have you heard something?"

"Some of my friends say Brebner parties are kind of wild."

"That's not true. None of my friends do drugs or anything."

Still, I hesitated to accept Barry's invitation. Would it be disloyal to Ainsley if I went to a party with someone else? "What is the matter, Caitlin?" Barry asked. "Do you have a boy-friend?"

"There is someone," I admitted, "but I don't usually see him at the weekend."

"Is he in boarding school?"

"Kind of."

"So," Barry said, "do you want to come to the regatta?"

I had made up my mind. A couple of meetings with Ainsley did not make him my boy-friend. "If you wait a minute, I'll go and ask Dad."

"Tell him I'll pick you up and bring you home afterwards."

My father was working at his computer and he pushed himself away from the desk. "Of course you can go to Barry's party, but tell him you have to be home by midnight."

"I'll give you a ring on Friday night," Barry promised, when I went back outside. "I might be able to borrow my mother's car again."

"I don't mind riding in your old bomb," I said. "You have my phone number, don't you?"

"You bet. It is casual, by the way. Just jeans."

As he walked to the car, I could not help thinking that Barry was so sure of himself, especially with his fancy car. And my mother would have said there was no harm in going out with different boys.

~~~

"I can't believe you have a date with Barry Egan-Smith," Ann said, her brown eyes flashing. "I told you about the parties that crowd has."

We were having lunch and I concentrated on opening a packet of tomato sauce. "I don't think Barry would do drugs when he is on the rowing team."

"What about alcohol?"

Gweneth leaned across the refectory table. "And kissing?"

"Where is the party?" Ann asked, ignoring

Gweneth.

"At Barry's home," I said.

"Are his parents going to be there?"

"Only his mother. His father lives in another state. I thought you knew all about him, Ann."

"I didn't say I knew anything about his family," Ann said.

"What are you going to wear?" Gweneth asked.

"Barry said to wear jeans," I replied.

"The other girls will be dressed up," Ann said. "I have a friend who went out with a senior boy last year. She said the other girls were very sophisticated."

"Caitlin is an American," Gweneth said. "She is sophisticated."

"What about Ainsley?" Ann asked.

"Ainsley won't mind," I said.

"I'll bet he'll be jealous," Gweneth said.

"Since you are going to the party, Caitlin," Ann said, "you should get a new outfit to wear. There's a lot of competition for Barry Egan-Smith."

I looked at Ann. "Do you think I can't handle competition?"

"I just don't want you to get hurt."

"I think Ainsley is the one who is going to get hurt," Gweneth said.

I was starting to feel annoyed with both Ann and Gweneth. "Ainsley won't know about the regatta."

"How do you know?" Gweneth said.

"My mother says you should only have one boy-friend at a time," Ann said.

"Ainsley is not my boy-friend," I said. "I have never even been on a date with him."

"You want to be careful, all the same." Ann's tone was instructing. "You will get the reputation for being wild."

"Honesty, Ann," I could not help saying, "you sound like something out of a Jane Austen novel."

After school, I went down to the willows to wait for Ainsley. I hung about for over an hour, but he never made an appearance. The afternoon turned cooler and I shivered in my short sleeves, hugging my arms tightly and wondering what could have happened to my friend. When the light began to fade, I finally went back into the house.

In my room, I took out Ainsley's sketch of my father's cottage and sat cross-legged on the bed, studying it. I was convinced that the sketch was real, and so was Ainsley. Why did he not come to meet me, as usual, at four o'clock?

CHAPTER 15

Another Visitor

In a burst of enthusiasm over my date with Barry, I tried on all the clothes in my closet. I finally decided to wear chinos and a wool blazer. At the dinner table, my father asked, "Do you need anything for your big day on Saturday?"

I did not like the way he said my "big day" as though it were my wedding day or something. Was my father trying to get rid of me, to have more time with Enid? "It is just a boat race, Dad."

"It would be nice for you to have someone like Barry to get about with."

"Barry doesn't have much spare time. He wants to get good grades so he can get into college."

"Good on him," my father said. "It is great to see a young chap with ambitions."

"Do you think it is good to have ambitions?" I asked.

"Of course it is. Barry has excellent prospects for the future."

I wondered what my father would say about

Ainsley's future prospects. "Do you think girls should have ambitions?" I asked.

"Girls can do anything boys can do," my father said. "I am sure you know that."

"Do you think I should go to college?"

"If you want to."

"I'm thinking about being a vet," I said.

"Then you will need to do well in science."

After dinner, my father went out to the shed to work on his old furniture, while I tackled my geometry homework in my room. I was reaching into my backpack when I heard a gentle scratching in the fireplace. Startled, I turned around, hearing the noise again. It was definitely coming from inside the hearth. The naughty possum must have dislodged the wire over the chimney.

Not wanting to frighten the little bush animal, I tip-toed across the room and knelt down on the tiles. I heard the scraping again, only louder this time. I had not used the fireplace, but it was still sooty, and I could not see inside the chimney without a flashlight.

"I am sorry if I disturbed you, Caitlin."

I swiveled around. "Ainsley!" The boy was sitting on the floor, just a few feet away from me. "I thought you were a possum!" I exclaimed. "Are you sure you didn't come down the chimney?"

Ainsley smiled, mischievously. "I might have."

I could not help smiling back, though my heart was pounding - not from fear, but because he had startled me. "There was a possum that came into the house."

"I often hear animals on the roof at night," Ainsley said.

I was still kneeling on the floor and I leaned back on my heels. "I waited for you yesterday. Where were you?"

"I know. I am sorry."

"Why didn't you meet me?"

"There were some other demands on my time," Ainsley said. "I hope you will accept my apology."

"I think it is time you met my father," I said. "He won't be angry that you are here, but you need to meet him."

Ainsley shook his head. "I cannot meet your father."

"Why not?"

"I came here to talk to you."

I could not let Ainsley make all the rules. "There was another boy here to see me on Sunday," I said.

"He didn't mind talking to my father."

Ainsley frowned. "Another boy? Who is he?"

"He is a friend," I said, quickly. "You need to understand that I can't keep seeing you without telling my father---."

"How old is this other boy?" Ainsley interrupted me.

"I don't know. About eighteen."

"Older than I am?"

"That isn't important," I said.

"Is he a gentleman?" Ainsley asked.

"I think so. You ask strange questions sometimes, Ainsley."

"I do?"

"Don't you know that?"

He looked away from me and shook his head. I instantly felt sorry I had hurt his feelings. "I had a really good time with you the other day."

"So did I," Ainsley said, smiling now.

"I don't want to be mean. I just want to understand you." I stopped. Ainsley was not wearing the digital watch. "What happened to your watch?"

"I do not wear a watch."

"But I gave you mine the other day."

Ainsley looked down at his wrist. "So you did. I had forgotten."

"What happened to it?" I repeated.

"I must have lost it somewhere."

The scratching in the fireplace started up again, distracting me. "There is still something caught in the chimney."

"Opossums come into the house to steal sugar," Ainsley said. "He will get himself out."

"Ainsley---?" I waited until I had his full attention. "Do you remember that drawing you did of my house?"

"Of course."

"It is beautiful, but there is something really strange about it. I found out that the artist died over a hundred years ago."

"That is ridiculous," Ainsley said. "Are you teasing me because I will not meet your father socially?"

"I would not tease you over something so serious," I replied.

"What is the matter?" Ainsley asked. "You can tell me. I will listen to you."

His eyes were very blue, and he was so close to me,

I was having difficulty concentrating on what I wanted to say. "All right. Does this house look the way it usually does to you?"

Ainsley shrugged. "I have not been inside the superintendent's house before."

I tried again. "When I look around, everything looks the way it is supposed to. But I don't think you and I are seeing the same things."

Ainsley was staring at me. "What do you mean?"

"What year is this?" I asked.

"You do think I am from the lunatic asylum. This is 1820."

"1820?" I whispered.

"Yes," Ainsley said, "1820."

"If it is 1820," I said, feeling like an actor in a play, "what year were you born?"

"In 1805," Ainsley said, forthrightly. "When were you born?"

"I was born in 1983, towards the end of the twentieth century." Outside my bedroom door, the house was silent, as though it were listening, too. I reminded myself that Ainsley was no older than I was, and he had not come into the house to harm me. "Don't you see? We are from different centuries. That is why you aren't wearing my watch. You couldn't bring it back with you."

Ainsley jumped to his feet. "Such a thing is against the laws of nature. When I find your watch, I will give it back and you can apologize to me."

I remembered the docent at the old inn telling me: "The trouble with ghosts is that they don't know they are ghosts." I stood up, too. "You won't find it because it is lost somewhere between your world and mine."

Ainsley went to the door and flung it open. "I have to leave."

"Wait! When will I see you again?"

In the hallway, Ainsley turned around to look at me and then he was gone, slamming the front door behind him.

"Caitlin!" My father was calling from the kitchen. "Is that you? I thought I heard something!"

"Yes, Dad," I shouted back. "It is only me."

CHAPTER 16

Some Revelations

Enid was waiting at the gate in her minivan when I came out of school the next day. She leaned over and opened the passenger door. "How was your day? I thought we could go back to my place for tea, if that is all right with you."

"Sure." I carefully put Ainsley's sketch on the seat beside me. "I hope you didn't mind that I called you last night."

"Of course not. I was pleased you thought of me to help with your problem."

Enid turned out of the school gates, heading west into the Blue Mountains. In the village of Glenbrook, she left the highway and drove down the dead-end street to her house, which was tucked away behind a tall hedge. On the front door was a sign reading, "Do not disturb! This means you!"

"I put out my sign when I'm painting," Enid explained.

"Aren't people offended by that?" I asked.

"People who know me understand. I don't worry about the others." Inside the house, Enid went about, throwing open the windows. "I am sorry about the smell of paint. Some days, this place is more like a studio than a home."

I looked at the empty easel by the window. "Are you working on anything?"

"I was. Would you like tea or coffee?"

I followed Enid into the kitchen. "Tea, thank you."

"Are you cold? I will close the windows in a minute."

I shook my head. "It doesn't seem cold after Boston."

"I know what you mean. I was like that when I came back from London." As soon as the kettle was boiling, Enid put the teapot and two cups on a tray with a plate of pastries. "I bought these in the village this morning. Have you had lamingtons before?"

"I don't think so."

"They are sponge cake dipped in chocolate icing." Enid carried the tea-tray into the living-room. "David tells me you have a date on Saturday."

I sat down on an overstuffed chair beside the fireplace. "It's not really a date. A boy from Brebner asked me to watch him row."

"That should be fun. Are you settling in at

Tennyson?"

"Kind of."

When I did not say any more, Enid wiped her hands on a cloth napkin. "You said you had something to show me."

Almost reluctantly, I passed Enid the drawing that Ainsley had done of my father's convict-built cottage. She unrolled the piece of parchment carefully. "This looks like your dad's house." Her eyebrows lifted. "Ainsley Allen?"

"Is it an original?" I asked, nervously.

"It's an original sketch. Is it really an Ainsley Allen?"

"Do you think it is?"

"It looks like his work," Enid said. "Where did you find this?"

"A boy I know gave it to me," I said. "You won't say anything about this to my dad, will you?"

Enid's eyes widened. "Who is this boy?"

"He is just a neighbor. He has been coming to see me after school."

"How old is he?"

I hesitated. "Fifteen or so."

"Do you know where he goes to school?" Enid

asked.

"He is home schooled."

"That is unusual here. Is he physically challenged or something?"

"I don't think so," I said. "He is quite handsome."

Enid was staring at me. "What is his name?"

I hesitated. "I am not sure."

"You might think I'm an old fuddy-duddy, but you should let David meet this young man." Enid took another look at Ainsley's drawing. "This is either an Ainsley Allen or a good forgery."

I remembered Ainsley's saying that his father had been convicted of forgery, but I had seen Ainsley sign his own name on the paper. "Why would someone forge a sketch like this?"

"For decorative purposes," Enid said, "or to make money."

"But my friend gave it to me."

"Maybe he is trying to impress you."

I stood up. "Could I have another look at that Allen painting in your gallery?"

"Of course. The owner hasn't decided whether he wants to sell it. It is the view from the escarpment near Mt. Riverview, looking down on Emu Plains,"

Enid added, when we were standing in front of the painting. "Allen went into areas that were fairly remote to paint his landscapes. He was quite 'avant-garde' for his time. It wouldn't have been easy to get about the bush in those days."

I studied the little watercolor again. It was the scene from the foothills where Ainsley and I had gone exploring together. I asked, faintly, "Do you know where he lived?"

"Along the Nepean River, judging from his paintings," Enid replied. "Historical records in the National Library show his father, or it may have been his grandfather, being sent to Australia on a transport ship."

"Do you think this is the same artist who drew my sketch?"

"Your sketch is more juvenile, the early work of a burgeoning talent. The watercolor was done by a more experienced artist."

I stared at Enid. "Are you saying Ainsley Allen was older when he painted the watercolor?"

"If your sketch is genuine."

"But you said he died young."

"A year or two can make a difference in an artist's style." Enid continued, as though giving a lecture, "Allen's work wasn't listed or sold until the 1940's.

We are still discovering pieces like this one, and lately the prices have gone through the roof."

My stomach felt queasy. Nothing that Enid had told me about Ainsley Allen fitted reality. "Can I use your phone, please? I have to call my father."

"There's no need to do that," Enid said. "I can drive you home."

"Right now?" I asked.

"If you like."

In the living-room, Enid watched me collect my back-pack and Ainsley's drawing. "You could leave the sketch here and I will get it appraised for you," she said. "The paper alone should tell us something about the work."

I shook my head. "My friend asked me not to show it to anyone. Thank you for the tea."

"Caitlin, can I say something?"

I waited politely.

"Sometimes," Enid said, "when we first meet a person, they have their guard down and we see them as they really are. What was your first impression of the boy who gave you that drawing?"

"I thought he was a pathological liar," I admitted. "I had a friend in Dallas like that."

Enid nodded. "If he keeps appearing at your

house, you really need to tell your father." She looked around. "Would you like to take some lamingtons home?"

CHAPTER 17

Partying

"I thought you liked Barry Egan-Smith," I said to my father. It was Saturday morning and we were having breakfast together.

"I do," he replied, "but you should know what to do if something happens when you are out with him. Some youngsters have too much money and not enough supervision."

"What could happen?"

"He might drink and drive, to begin with."

"There won't be alcohol at the regatta. It is a school thing."

But my dad had the last word. "If there are drugs or alcohol at the party, ring me up straight away and I'll come and get you."

Barry picked me up from my home in his battered old car. I did not see much of him during the races on the river except in the skull, but he came looking for me when the regatta was over. He was wearing a tracksuit in his school colors and his hair was dripping wet.

"I'm sorry I took so long, Caitlin," he said. "We had some work to do at the boathouse. Has it been too boring for you?"

I pushed my hands into my pockets. "I sat with some Tennyson girls. We cheered your team as hard as we could."

"Too bad we didn't win." Barry unlocked his car and tossed his duffel bag on to the back seat. "Let's go and get some hamburgers."

"Is the party still on?" I asked.

"Of course, but the others won't be arriving at the house for a while. You're not nervous about coming home with me, are you?"

"Will your mother be there?"

"Mother has gone to Surfers Paradise for a couple of days," Barry replied. "That's up north in Queensland."

"I went to friends' houses in Dallas when their parents were out-of-town," I said. "It is no big deal."

"Great."

We stopped at a restaurant on the way to Barry's house for take-out 'burgers and chips, or "take away", as he called it. I did not mention that I was vegetarian. "I'll pay for mine," I offered.

"It's my shout," Barry said. "Anyway, a gentleman always pays for a lady."

It was getting dark by the time we turned into Barry's driveway. The one-story house was large and sprawling, and beautifully decorated. The foyer was paved with black-and-white marble tiles and the windows in the living-room soared up to the ceiling, framing a view across the Nepean River.

Barry led me into the kitchen, where he put the hamburgers on the table. He opened the refrigerator and took out a bottle of champagne. "Mum locks up her best glasses." He reached into the cupboard for some tumblers. "We could drink to the losers."

"To Brebner." I politely took a sip of champagne and then put down the cup.

"Brebner will win next time," Barry said. "Don't you like champagne?"

"I'm not used to drinking alcohol," I said.

Barry grinned. "I'm not sure it goes with hamburgers anyway."

"This is a beautiful house," I said, gazing around.

"When I'm a pediatrician," Barry said, "I'll be able to afford a house like this, but with a pool. Mum won't get one because she says they are too much work."

"Do you want to be a doctor so you can make money?" I asked.

Barry shrugged. "My parents will pay my way, if I go to uni'. Whenever I talk about what I am going to do, they always say, 'Well, you could be a doctor, or a lawyer, or a vet.'"

"I want to be a vet," I confided.

"Do you? I can't picture someone like you treating cows and horses."

My cheeks felt warm. I wondered if it were possible to get drunk on just one sip of champagne. "Do you mind if we go outside?" I asked. "I think I need some fresh air."

Barry immediately jumped up and opened the sliding glass door to the patio. I felt much better outside in the breeze, and the view was worth looking at. Moonlight gleamed on the river and the western bank was dotted with the lights of Emu Plains.

"The Nepean is the same river as the Hawkesbury," Barry said, "but the early explorers thought they'd found another river. That is why it has two names." He stopped. "You are very pretty, Caitlin. You know that, don't you?"

"Am I?"

"That chap you usually go out with, where is he tonight?"

"I don't know," I said. "We are not going steady or anything." I had been thinking about Ainsley, too, as I looked across the river. Was he wandering along the creek waiting for me, or was he skipping across the stars?

Barry took my hand in a proprietary way. Just then, someone called out, "Hey, Barry, how's tricks?"

"We've been ringing your door-bell for ages," someone else shouted.

Barry's friends came through the side gate to the patio and he dropped my hand and went to meet them. One boy was carrying a carton of beer and the other had a flagon of wine under his arm. Barry introduced us. "Caitlin, this is Craig and Terry and Julie and Michelle."

"Isn't this a great house?" one of the girls said, tossing her long hair like a pony. "Lucky Barry has it all to himself for the weekend. I brought that dip you like, Barry, and salt-and-vinegar chips."

Barry took his friends into the house and I followed them. They were all laughing at some private joke I did not understand. In the kitchen, the boys started passing cans of beer around and opening the wine. I had liked being alone with Barry, but a choir had not started singing in my ears or anything, the way it was supposed to. How could it, when I had been thinking about Ainsley the whole day? I excused myself and went down the hallway to the powder room. I looked at my reflection in the mirror over the sink. My hair was messed up and my eyes looked over-bright.

By the time I went back to the living room, the music was blaring and someone had dimmed the lights. More of Barry's friends had arrived and they were helping themselves to drinks. I found Barry out on the patio where he and Michelle were passing a cigarette back and forth to each other. I had known people in Dallas who smoked "pot" and I recognized the peculiar smell in the air: marijuana.

Barry gave me a silly smile. "There you are, Katie. Would you like a drag?"

I stared at him. "My name is Caitlin. I didn't know there would be drugs at your party."

"I thought you'd be used to drugs, coming from the States."

"Not everyone in America does drugs."

"How about more champagne?" Barry asked.

"You are an athlete," I said. "How can you do that to yourself?"

"I don't want a lecture," Barry said. "I get enough of those from my parents."

"What grade are you in at school, Caitlin?"

Michelle asked, sweetly. "Kindergarten?"

An insistent voice in my head was asking, "What are you doing here?" I knew my dad would want me to leave the party. My mother would have added, "But don't make a fuss about it."

I went into the hallway and picked up the phone. I was waiting at the front door when Barry came looking for me. "What are you doing?"

"I am going home," I said.

"Is someone coming for you?" he asked, sounding genuinely concerned.

"My father," I said, shortly.

"Are you jealous of Michelle? You know that is silly. When will I see you again?"

"I don't know. Maybe at the school dance." I watched the headlights of a car turning into the driveway. I had never been so pleased to see my father's old station-wagon.

"Is everything all right?" my father asked, swinging open the passenger door.

I sank into the well-worn leather seat. "Everything is fine. Can we just leave?"

CHAPTER 18

Liberation

"Wake up, Australia! How was your date with Barry Egan-Smith?"

I was so engrossed in my own thoughts, Ann's voice startled me. "Brebner lost the regatta."

"We don't care about the silly regatta. We want to know if you're going out with Barry again."

"I don't think so," I said.

Gweneth leaned across the library table. "Isn't he romantic?"

"Not really."

Ann smiled. "She's lying."

"No, I'm not," I protested. "What you said about those boys and their parties is true."

"They are too old for us," Ann said.

Gweneth said, "I played tennis at the weekend with my cousin."

"I went to the pictures with a boy I knew from primary school," Ann said.

"Did you have a good time?" I asked.

"It was all right. Have you seen Ainsley again?"

"No."

"Why don't you go and see him?" Ann said. "He lives near you, doesn't he?"

Gweneth said, "We are liberated now. A girl can ask a boy out any time she wants."

"You are the American girl, aren't you?"

I looked up. "Yes, Miss Gordon."

The school librarian put a book down on the table. "This might be what you were looking for. It has a chapter on everyday life in the 1820's. The due-date is stamped inside."

"Thank you, Miss Gordon," I said.

"Are you trying to win the history prize, Caitlin?" Ann asked.

"What history prize?"

"They announce the prizes at Speech Night at the end of the year for every subject. We wear white dresses, and the parents are invited."

"Ann won a prize for English last year," Gweneth said.

Ann shrugged. "They just give you a book like 'Wuthering Heights' or something."

~ ~ ~

I knew Ann and Gweneth were right. There was no reason I should not make the first move with Ainsley. At home, I searched in my wardrobe for the calico skirt and blouse I had worn on History Day. Putting them on, I studied myself in the mirror and decided that I did look like a girl from the past. If Ainsley came back, I would not scare him away again by talking about missing watches. I would just be pleased that I was with him.

Down at the creek, I sat on the grass and spread my old-fashioned skirt around me, feeling a little nervous. I had been waiting for about half-an-hour when I heard footsteps behind me. I swung around. There was something different about Ainsley today. His hair was longer, but it was more than that. His face was less rounded, his features more defined. And he was taller than I remembered him.

"Do you like me a little older, Caitlin?" he asked, smiling.

I had not seen Ainsley for about two weeks. How could he be much older? I scrambled to my feet. "I do. I mean, it doesn't matter to me how old you are."

"You look beautiful," Ainsley said.

"I wore this the first time we met, but it isn't how I usually dress."

"Because you are from America."

I wanted to say, "Because I am from the twentieth century." Instead, I said, "What have you been doing?"

Ainsley said, solemnly, "I have been working on sketches of native animals and birds. So far, I have completed the koala and the kangaroo."

"Will I get to see them?"

"When they are all finished."

"What about your father?" I asked. "Does he know?"

Ainsley looked surprised. "I suppose he does. He has been ill since last winter. He developed a lung complaint after the floods."

"I am sorry. What floods?"

"Did you not know about that? The water comes down from the Warragamba River and floods the valley. I have to help run the farm nowadays."

I stared at him for a moment. "I don't believe you are helping with the farm, Ainsley."

"Why is that?"

"Because you are so clean and neat. I stayed at a friend's ranch once in Mexico, and my clothes were covered in dust the whole time."

Ainsley was standing close to me and there was nothing ghost-like about his warm young body.

Suddenly, I did not care where he had been all this time. Almost instinctively, I leaned towards him and he put his arms around me as though that was where I belonged. I closed my eyes and I could smell the soap his shirt had been laundered in, and the crisp aroma of burning eucalyptus leaves. Everything around us was quiet. The only sound I could hear was Ainsley's steady breathing and the crunch of the dry grass under my feet. And his kiss was soft and gentle, almost shy, the first step on a journey of discovery. I said, breathlessly, "I have never been kissed like that before."

"Do you want me to kiss you again?" Ainsley asked.

"I don't know. This is kind of scary."

"Aren't you happy that we are finally together?"

I thought the word "finally" sounded strange, but I did not want to spoil the moment by asking questions. "I am very happy we are together."

"Then come with me, Caitlin. I will show you my new mare, and the homestead where I was born. There is nothing to keep you here," Ainsley went on. "You have not been able to make strong attachments to anyone."

"That is only because I miss my mother," I said, trying to be sensible. "I will get over it, in time."

Ainsley was holding my hand tightly. "Time isn't the problem, or the solution."

I looked back towards my house. My father would not be home for a couple of hours. Why not go with Ainsley to his house? There was really nothing to keep me here.

"Caitlin!" Enid was calling to me from the other side of the fence.

"Someone is looking for me," I said. "I am sorry, Ainsley, but I have to go."

"Caitlin!" Edith called again.

Ainsley insisted, "Come with me. It will be much more fun."

The breeze felt cold on my neck and a shiver went down my spine. I was still holding his hand. "Where are we going?" I asked.

"We are going home."

Ainsley and I crossed the parched creek bed together and then suddenly I realized that we were on the other side of the river. "Don't let go of my hand," I said, "or you will lose me."

"We are nearly there," Ainsley said, sounding amused.

I looked around. We had come to a little stone

cottage, hardly larger than my father's house. Despite being so small, the cottage had three chimneys, but some of the wooden roof had fallen in, and parts of the stone walls had been destroyed. I took a deep breath. "Is this where you live, Ainsley?"

"Do you like it?" Ainsley asked.

"Yes, but it looks very old."

"The cottage is quite new."

"That is odd," I said. "Is this where you grew up?"

"No," Ainsley said, "this is just a sheep-run."

"For Merino sheep?" I asked. "Are they raised for wool?"

"I do not like that either, but animals should definitely not be bred to eat."

I stared at him. "Are you a vegetarian?"

"What is that?" Ainsley asked.

"A person who doesn't eat meat," I said.

"Are you a vegetarian?" he asked.

"Yes."

"Then I am, too."

I smiled at him, feeling a little more relaxed. "Are there any horses in the stables?"

"Do you like horses?" Ainsley asked, surprised.

"Of course. I am from Texas."

We walked through the long grass to the barn, but there were no animals there, or in the dilapidated stables, or anywhere else that I could see. Ainsley was watching me closely. "My family owns this land. I wanted to share it with you."

Visiting the deserted farm with Ainsley felt strange, but I reminded myself that it was still daylight and I was not far from home. If I had to, I could take the train across the Nepean River to Emu Plains. "Does your family have another property? You said you used to live in Parramatta."

"Did I?"

"Could I see the other house?" I asked. "Is it far from here?"

He thought for a moment. "Very well."

The blue sky seemed to cloud over a little as we walked to the top of the rise behind the stables. The dirt road ahead led us through brick gateposts and up to a large ranch-style house with a flagstone verandah. Were we in Parramatta already? I was getting used to these sudden changes in scenery, but I had to exclaim, "Ainsley, what a beautiful house. Is anyone living here?"

"I doubt it. I usually have this place to myself."

"What about your family?"

"I don't want anyone else to be here," Ainsley admitted, "except you, of course."

"Can we go on to the verandah?" I asked.

"I suppose so. "

"You talked about your father," I could not help reminding him.

"That was a long time ago." Ainsley was walking restlessly back and forth over the flagstones. "We used to play hopscotch here."

I could feel a sudden chill in the air, but this time Ainsley seemed unaware that the day was coming to an end. "Who did you play with?" When he did not answer me, I said, "Could we take a look inside?"

"There is nothing inside," Ainsley said.

"I would like to look at the rooms."

"I am sorry," Ainsley said, seriously, "but I cannot take you inside."

"Don't you have a key?" I asked.

He shook his head.

"Then we had better go back to Emu Plains," I said. "It is getting late and I have homework. Won't someone be looking for you?" When Ainsley did not answer me, I went on, "Do you really remember playing on this verandah?"

"I remember what I choose to remember," Ainsley replied. "I wish you could stay with me a little longer."

For some reason, the aroma of honeysuckle hung in the air, but there were no vines that I could see. It would be getting dark soon and I could imagine my father worrying and wondering where I was. "I will stay longer another day," I promised.

Before I could even consider being trapped here for the night, I was standing beside the weeping willow and looking at my home. Sebastian was waiting on the doorstep, but Ainsley had disappeared.

CHAPTER 19

More Tea

"Are you all right, Caitlin?" Enid called, from the kitchen door.

I closed the wooden gate behind me. I did not dare look back over my shoulder to see if Ainsley was standing amongst the willows. "I have been looking for Sebastian," I told her.

Sebastian had run into the house ahead of me. Enid was looking curiously at me. "Why are you wearing those old-fashioned clothes?"

I brushed the hair out of my eyes. "I am in a play at school," I lied. "We are doing 'A Christmas Carol.'"

"Interesting. What part do you have?"

"Mrs. Crotchit."

"Mrs. Cratchit?"

"That's it," I said.

"I am cooking dinner tonight," Enid said. "Did your father tell you? I thought I would make fried rice and prawns. I bought the prawns already cooked and peeled, but you probably won't want any."

I said, distantly, "I'll just have rice and vegetables.

If you don't mind, I'll go and get changed."

"I'll make us a cup of tea."

I went to my bedroom and closed the door. My hands were trembling as I took off the colonial clothes and put on my jeans and sweater. In my head, I could still hear Ainsley's voice saying, "There is nothing to keep you here."

When I went back to the kitchen, Enid had a saucepan simmering on the stove and she had made a pot of tea. I sat down at the table and asked, trying to sound casual, "Are you going to live here after you and Dad are married?"

"I suppose so," Enid said. "We haven't really talked about that."

"What about your gallery?"

"I plan to keep it open, and I will still use my house as a studio." Enid added, picking up the teapot, "I didn't know they had predicted rain this afternoon."

The sound of sudden heavy drops on the iron roof over our heads was almost deafening. "Someone told me it floods out here," I said.

"It used to, before they built the Warragamba Dam." Enid opened her tote bag and took out a brown paper packet. "I brought you this from the gallery."

"You didn't have to give me anything," I began.

"You seemed so interested in Ainsley Allen's work, I ordered some prints. I have a set of Australian animals - and this one. I thought you might like it."

Ainsley had talked about sketching the native animals. As I unwrapped Enid's present, I caught a glimpse of the drawing inside the packet and my tea went spilling across the kitchen table. Enid jumped up and grabbed a kitchen towel. "Did it go on you? Are you burned?"

"No, I'm okay." I could feel my bottom lip starting to tremble. "I am sorry."

"Don't apologize. There is no damage done."

I was still holding the little print. It was a replica of the sketch Ainsley had done of me in the hills, only in pen and ink. It was my profile, looking back towards him, and he had made me look very pretty. "This is me."

Enid went back to the kitchen sink. "It certainly looks like you."

"No, I mean it is me. Ainsley did a sketch of me that day we went into the bush." I stopped, and managed to stammer, "It is very nice. Thank you."

"I am glad you like it, dear." Enid turned around to look at me. "I have been thinking that you spend a lot of time on your own."

"It's all right," I said, still looking at Ainsley's drawing. "I usually have homework."

"Have you thought about doing something after school, apart from homework? There is a heated pool in Emu Plains, if you like to swim."

"I don't like heated pools."

"You could take piano lessons, or tennis," Enid said.

"I can play tennis."

"Then we should find a game for you with other young people."

I said, not looking at Enid, "I am okay."

"That boy you told me about, is he still bothering you?"

"He doesn't bother me. I might not see him again, anyway."

"Why not?" Enid asked.

I did not like Enid's questions, or the way she had taken over the kitchen as though she belonged there. "Because Ainsley is a spirit," I said.

Enid came back to the table. "Why do you say that?"

"He thinks he is in the nineteenth century."

I put Ainsley's sketch on the table between us.

Enid said, looking down at it, "You are convinced he is Ainsley Allen, aren't you?"

I took a deep breath. "I know he is. That drawing I have in my closet - the one I showed you - you can do any test on it that you like. The signature is real and the paper is over a hundred years old. I am not crazy, Enid."

"I don't think you are crazy," Enid said, firmly, "but if your friend is a ghost - and that is a big 'if' - what is he doing in your backyard?"

"Land along the Nepean River was part of his father's farm."

"Caitlin, you are very intelligent and imaginative."

"I am not imagining any of this," I said, stubbornly.

"Of course not," Enid said, "but we still have to consider all possibilities. Being confronted by something like this doesn't happen every day of the week, at least not to me."

"It doesn't to me, either."

"What does this spirit want?"

"Why should he want something?" I asked.

"He must have a reason for haunting the place," Enid insisted. "Have you asked him why he isn't able to rest?"

"Ainsley doesn't know he is a ghost. He was confused when he saw me wearing my colonial costume on History Day. He thought I was part of his world."

"If he is a ghost," Enid said, "his world has long since gone. He should have gone, too. What is keeping him here?"

"His art," I said.

"Why would that keep him here?"

"Because his work was never appreciated when he was alive." I knew my voice was getting louder. "No one encouraged him to paint or draw and he is still working on being a successful artist."

"Do you think you are in any danger from being around him?" Enid asked.

"From Ainsley? Of course not."

"Why do you say you won't be seeing him again?"

"Because he comes and goes in his own way," I said.

"And you haven't told your father about this?" Enid said.

"It is too weird to explain," I said.

"You explained it to me."

"You are different. We are not related, and you

are a painter."

Enid smiled, gravely. "I must say it is a romantic story, a young artist who has given beauty to the world, but can't find peace after death because he was not fulfilled when he was alive."

"If I am making up stories, explain this." I nodded towards Ainsley's sketch.

The rain was still pounding on the roof. Enid leaned over and gave me an awkward hug. "You are missing your mother. That might be why you are thinking about ghosts and spirits."

I drew away from her. "Ainsley has nothing to do with my mother."

The rice on the stove was boiling over, but Enid ignored it. "I think we need more tea," she said.

CHAPTER 20

The Beach

Next day at school, Miss Shock called me into her office. "Your father rang me this morning, Caitlin. He says you are going away for a holiday together."

I stared at the headmistress. "Where are we going?"

"I thought you knew about it. He is taking you to the beach for a short break."

"What about my school work?" I asked.

"You will be gone for less than a fortnight," Miss Shock said. "Your father thinks it is important for you to get away right now because of your mother's anniversary, as I understand."

"That is over two months away. Please, could I call - could I ring him now?"

"I think it might be better to wait and talk to your father at home."

"I need to talk to him now," I pleaded.

"Very well," Miss Shock said, "you can use my phone, but please make it as short as possible."

"Yes, Miss Shock." The antique store was closed on Tuesdays, but my father would probably be there, working on his inventory. As I dialed his number on the old black telephone, my thoughts were tumbling over one another. Was he really taking me on a vacation because it was the anniversary of my mother's death? Or had Enid been talking to him about my problem with Ainsley?

At the other end of the phone, my father's voice was crisp. "This is David Pritchard."

"Dad, this is Caitlin."

"Caitlin?" As always, he sounded like a boy through the phone. "Are you at school?"

"Yes, I am in Miss Shock's office. She says you want to take me out of school."

"That's right."

"I need to know what is going on, Dad."

"Nothing to worry about. We haven't spent much time together and I thought it was time we did. I have booked a flat at the beach for a week or so, that's all."

"Is Enid coming with us?"

"No," my father said, "Enid is going to look after the shop. Can we talk about this at home, Caitlin?"

"Why are we going to the beach now? It will be too cold to swim."

"The beach is a great place in the winter. We can light a fire, toast marshmallows---"

"I don't want to go away right now," I interrupted.

"Why not? Most kids would love to have a holiday at this time of year."

"You don't understand," I said. "I'm just starting to settle in at school."

"I don't think a week on the south coast is going to ruin your school work," my father said, sounding amused. "Miss Shock agrees with me."

"What about Sebastian? Who is going to look after him?"

"Enid says she will come by and feed him twice a day."

Enid was going to be busy. I put down the phone. "Could I make another call, Miss Shock?"

Miss Shock sighed. "Really, Caitlin---"

"Please, it is very important."

"Do you have the number?"

I shook my head. Reluctantly, Miss Shock pushed the telephone book across the desk. I ran through the listings until I found Enid's name. The phone rang a couple of times before the answering machine picked up my call, so I put down the phone. In a way, it was just as well. If Enid had answered, I would not have known what to say.

~~~

The beach south of Sydney, near Stanwell Park, was a gorgeous place, and the apartment my father had rented was right on the water. From the front room, I watched the ships passing on the horizon, and at night I could hear the surf breaking on the sand. In the afternoon when the tide was out, blue lagoons formed along the shoreline.

Every morning, my father went jogging along the beach. After the first day, I decided to go with him. I enjoyed the run along the sand and on the way home we stopped at the neighborhood "deli" to have milk-shakes served in vintage metal containers. In the evening, we fished in the surf, standing knee-deep in the foaming water, but I was grateful that we never caught anything.

One afternoon, we were strolling along the beach, when my father said, "Enid tells me you have met a strange young man near the house."

The wind was blowing in our faces and I pulled my coat around me. "Ainsley isn't strange, Dad. He is a nice boy."

My father was looking serious. "Doesn't he think he is a ghost or something?"

"Enid shouldn't have told you that."

He waited as the seagulls squawked over our heads. "I know I haven't been at home as much as I should. It isn't fair to leave you on your own every day."

"I don't mind being on my own," I said. "I thought you believed in a spirit world."

"I don't think spirits wander about amongst the living, talking to us. If your friend told you that, he is either a half-wit or a liar."

I stood still. "I don't want to walk any further, Dad."

My father turned back to me, his expression still serious. "You must know what this boy told you is a load of rubbish. I would rather you didn't see him again."

"I can't talk to you about this." I said.

"Then maybe you should talk to someone outside the family."

"You mean a psychiatrist? Do you think I am imagining things?"

"Of course not. I have a friend who is a therapist. She could recommend someone for us."

I knew my face was getting red. "You've already made an appointment for me, haven't you?"

"I thought we could go together. This is mostly

my fault. Here you are, still grieving for your mother, and I leave you alone in that depressing old house."

"I don't need a psychiatrist."

But my father went on, "Miss Shock mentioned a very good boarding school in Sydney. They can't take you this year, but they will have a place for you in February."

I could not believe what I was hearing. "You're going to send me away to boarding school?"

"You won't be that far away, and your time will be better organized for you. You can come home every weekend."

"Aunt Natalie promised you wouldn't send me to boarding school." The breeze from the sea was blowing hard, but it was almost comforting to feel the cold wind on my face.

"Your aunt shouldn't have made a promise like that."

"You and Enid want to get rid of me," I interrupted. "I am just a nuisance to you."

"You are not a nuisance. I am thinking about boarding school for your own good."

"Adults always say that when they are doing something mean," I flung at him. I turned around and headed back to the apartment. When I reached the block of flats, I looked back over my shoulder. My father was still on the beach, watching some children playing with buckets and spades in the wet sand. I went into the apartment and slammed the door. There was no one else to hear, but it made me feel better.

CHAPTER 21

Cold

My first impulse was to pack my bags, get out on the road, and hitch-hike back to Emu Plains. But common sense told me that would be a stupid thing to do. My father must have known he had ruined our vacation because, a little later, he came back to the apartment and announced, quite calmly, that we would be going home to Emu Plains a few days early.

"That's okay with me," I said. "I didn't want to come here in the first place."

He gave me a long look, but all he said was, "We can leave after lunch tomorrow."

~ ~ ~

Sebastian came running down the hallway to meet us when we arrived back home. The cottage was gloomy and cold and my father quickly opened the blinds and turned on the oil heater.

In my room, everything looked just the way I had left it, and there were no sooty footprints along the fireplace. I unpacked my suitcase and tossed my clothes into the laundry basket. My school bag was lying in the corner and I wondered if Miss Shock expected me to finish my homework from the previous week.

My father was already talking on the phone to Enid. Not wanting to listen to their conversation, I opened the back door and went into the garden. I could not help looking over the fence, though I knew Ainsley never came by on Wednesdays, for some reason.

"Caitlin!"

My father was standing on the porch. "Enid would like to talk to you."

Reluctantly, I went to the telephone.

"Caitlin, how are you, dear?" Enid said.

"I'm fine, thank you," I said.

"Did you enjoy your holiday?"

"It was all right."

"I know you are angry with me for telling David about Ainsley," Enid said.

"It doesn't matter," I replied. "He doesn't believe the story, anyway."

"What if something were to happen to you because of this boy? It would be irresponsible of me not to tell your dad."

"I know. It is for my own good."

"I just want to help, if I can."

"Do you want to talk to Dad again?"

There was a short silence. "All right," Enid said. "Put him back on the line."

That night, I sat up in bed, reading Australian history and listening for the possums on the roof. Shivering, I wondered where Ainsley went when he was not with me. Did he go back to an old graveyard, or was there somewhere else he was supposed to be? I really had little say in what Ainsley did, one way or another. He was following his own destiny with or without me.

~~~

I had caught a cold at the beach and I was forced to stay home from school the next day.

"If you don't need the doctor," my father said, solicitously, "can I get you anything from the chemist shop?"

"You could bring me another box of tissues," I said.

"I'll give you a ring later on. I can come home early, if you need me."

As soon as my father had left the house, I took a blanket and pillows and settled down on the sofa in the living-room. Later, I would try to finish my homework. I must have dropped off to sleep, for the sharp ringing of the phone startled me into consciousness. Thinking it was my father, I took my time answering it.

"Miss Pritchard?"

"This is Caitlin Pritchard."

"My name is John McAllister," the caller said. "You don't know me, but I know your father from the antique store. One of the ladies at the museum said you wanted some information about an old grave."

My mouth went dry. "That's right. I'm looking for the grave---for the graves of a family named Allen."

"Are you still in school?"

"Yes; but I'm having a sick day."

"I've been doing some research for a book I am writing." Mr. McAllister sounded elderly, and self-important. "I haven't found anything in Emu Plains, but there are people named Allen buried in Windsor."

"Windsor?" My heart sank. Why would Ainsley be buried in Windsor?

"You are an American, aren't you?" Mr. McAllister asked. "Windsor is a small town on the Hawkesbury River, north of Emu Plains. A beautiful church was built there in colonial days, St. Matthew's, designed by

Francis Greenway. It has a very old cemetery. Ask one of your friends to take you there and look in the northwest corner of the grounds."

I knew Francis Greenway was a famed convict architect in Governor Macquarie's time. I said, weakly, "Thank you, Mr. McAllister. I appreciate your help."

"No trouble, girlie. Good luck."

I put down the phone. My father's antique store was in Windsor. Was I about to learn more about Ainsley and his family, or would this be a wild goose chase, as my grandmother used to say?

CHAPTER 22

To: "Dr. Tim Robbins" <timrob@onramp.net>

Subject: Family news

Aunt Natalie, Uncle Tim, Marybeth, Alicia, and Peter,

The weather is still cold here, but nothing like a Boston winter. I think I would miss the snow if I stayed here long.

Dad and I went to the beach for a few days, but it was too cold to swim. He is talking about sending me to another school next year, to boarding school. Has he told you anything about it? I think it is a terrible idea. What do you think?

I did all right in the exams, except for French. I will never be able to go to France.

Hope you are all well. Please e-mail me and tell me what you think about boarding schools.

Thank you for the candy.

Love, Caitlin.

CHAPTER 23

Surprises

"If you feel up to it, Caitlin," my father said, "you could come to the shop with me tomorrow. Miss Shock doesn't expect you back at school until Monday."

I could not believe it was so easy to get to Windsor. I would be able to search for the graves Mr. McAllister had told me about. "I wasn't looking forward to going back to school tomorrow," I said.

"Why is that?" my father asked, suspiciously.

"I don't want to explain to everyone why we came home early from the beach."

He leaned back in his arm-chair. It was evening and we were sitting in front of the television set, watching the news. "You might like to have a look around Windsor while you are there."

I propped myself up on one elbow. "Did you mean what you said about sending me away to school?"

"Boarding school isn't like reform school. It would be like going away to college."

"But did you mean it?"

"We'll see," was all he would say.

~~~

My father was proud of his antique store in Windsor, with its old-style store front and the name, "Panning for Gold," hanging on a swinging sign. While he fussed with the lights and the cash register, I made a pot of coffee in the little kitchen. "I am glad to see you're feeling better," he said.

"Later on," I said, "I might go for a walk around the town."

"You could get some lunch for us while you're out."

I liked being at the store, especially looking through the clothes. But business was slow and by mid-morning, I said, "I think I'll go for a walk and look at the courthouse and the church."

"I'm sorry I can't come with you," my father said. "St. Matthew's is just up the hill." He smiled. "Don't talk to any strangers."

Though the day was sunny, my throat felt scratchy, so I put on my jacket and scarf. "I'll pick up some sandwiches on the way back," I promised.

I had seen a photograph of St. Matthew's Church in the local newspaper with its mellow red bricks and round bell tower, and in my history book. The simple country church, part of Australia's past, sat sedately on a hill overlooking the town. In the southwest corner of the churchyard, I had no problem finding the graves that John McAllister had told me about. They belonged to a husband and wife named Richard and Joan Allen, who had both died in 1896. That was too late into the nineteenth century to have anything to do with Ainsley.

Though I wandered through the rest of the cemetery, I could not find anyone else named Allen buried there. The door of the church was open and, in my imagination, I could almost see the colonial gentlemen and their ladies filing into the pews. I stepped into the cool, dark sanctuary for a moment, and I was blinking outside in the sunshine again when I heard a familiar voice. "Hello, Caitlin."

I stood still. "Ainsley! What are you doing here?"

He was sitting on an elevated stone tomb, dressed in a velvet jacket with his white shirt open at the neck. "Waiting for you, ma'am." He pronounced the word, "ma'arm."

"How did you know I would be here?" I asked, astonished.

"I knew you would come searching for me sooner or later. Come and sit beside me, just to be near me."

"I can't sit on someone's grave," I began.

Ainsley grinned mischievously. "You do not believe the gentleman is still here, do you? He is long since gone. All these people have gone. This was a burial ground years before the new church was built."

"How do you know?"

"I just know."

"We could go and sit in the church," I suggested.

"I do not care much for churches." Ainsley jumped down on to the path beside me. "May I kiss you?"

"I've had a head cold," I began. "Maybe you shouldn't get too close."

"I don't care about that. Have you missed me?"

"I didn't think I would ever see you again," I admitted.

"Did you not know I would come back for you?" Ainsley put his arms out to me and I had no choice but to let them close around me. When he kissed me, all the waiting and wondering no longer mattered. Our lips finally separated and I rested my head on his shoulder. "I've had enough of the cemetery," I said. "Could we go for a walk somewhere - maybe down to the river?"

He was stroking my hair. "We cannot go down to the river. When the river was in flood, I tried to help a farmer and his family. The boat capsized and they all drowned."

My heart gave an awful thud. Was this what had happened? Had Ainsley drowned in the river? "Did you fall into the river, too?"

Ainsley did not answer me directly. "They found the others, but they did not find me. I lost my sketchbox."

"You don't need your sketchbox, Ainsley. You don't have to do any more painting."

"Of course I have to paint. My work is still frivolous and juvenile."

I looked up at him. "Your work is finished here. You have to believe that, or you'll never have any peace---."

"I don't want peace," he interrupted me. "No one knows my work. I have yet to be recognized as an artist."

"But you should not be hanging around here."

"If you were with me, I would not stay here." Ainsley's voice had risen with excitement. "I could be happy with you."

"Are you sure that is the way it works?" I asked, doubtfully.

"There are no rules. We make our own destiny."

I touched his sleeve. The fabric of his jacket felt

soft and expensive. An awful thought came to me. These might have been his burial clothes. "Do you have a grave? Or is that why you can't rest? We could find some stones and flowers and make you a grave."

"I need to finish my work," Ainsley said. "Come back to my home with me. I can draw and paint and you can be my helpmate."

The trees around us began to rustle their leaves, as though in chorus. Ainsley was still holding my hand, but now his palm felt cold and dry. I knew the answer I had to give him. "I can't do that, Ainsley."

"Why not?" he asked.

"Because there are so many things I still want to do," I said. "Your life in this world is complete, but mine is just beginning."

"Are you afraid of me?"

"No, but I'm kind of afraid for you. I want you to go where you are supposed to be." I tried to remember what Enid had told me about Ainsley's art. "You don't have to worry about your work. Your paintings and drawings bring thousands of dollars--- English pounds---in my century."

"Which paintings?" Ainsley asked, sharply. "What are you talking about?"

The wintry sun that had been shining so valiantly began to fade. "I mean your landscapes, and the sketches you did of the koala and the other animals. They are hanging in galleries everywhere. You are a successful artist almost two hundred years after you were born. You can leave without looking back at anything or anyone."

"What you are telling me about my work," Ainsley said, "is that the truth?"

"Of course it is. Why would I lie to you?" I knew my voice was trembling. "All your dreams have come true."

He let go of my hand. "If my life is complete, that means going on by myself." He sounded surprisingly calm. "I suppose I should go back to the river."

I looked behind me at the red brick church. I was blinking back tears, but I had to be sensible. "I don't think you will have to go to the river. Just go into the church."

"Is that what you want me to do?"

"Yes, Ainsley, that is what I want you to do."

"Kiss me one last time?" he asked.

I put my arms around his neck and he gave me a last, sweet kiss and then he was gone, walking quickly across the grass to the door of the church. As I had predicted, he did not look back. I felt the sudden stillness around me, then the birds in the trees started chirping all at once, cars drove noisily passed on the street, and a bus-load of tourists arrived. Feeling oddly elated, I picked up the scarf I had dropped on the path and hurried towards the gate.

CHAPTER 24

Call to Boston

Halfway around the world, in Boston, Aunt Natalie answered the telephone. "Caitlin, is that you?"

"Yes, it's me, Aunt Natalie."

"What a nice surprise. How are you, dear?"

"I'm okay. Did you get my e-mail?"

"Of course we did."

"Then you know Dad wants to send me to boarding school."

The delay on the line was longer than usual. Aunt Natalie said, "Caitlin, there might be some advantages for you - going to a school like that. You would have the company of other boarders."

"I have made some friends at Tennyson," I said. "You promised I wouldn't have to go away to school."

"We didn't know your dad's situation then."

"You've already talked to him about this, haven't you?"

"We all have your interests at heart," Aunt Natalie said. "David said you were getting some counseling."

"I went to counseling," I said. "The therapist said there is nothing wrong with me."

"Hold on a moment, Caitlin. I'll get Uncle Tim."

"I don't want to talk---" I began.

But my uncle was already on the line. "Hi, Caitlin. How's it going?"

"I want to come back to Boston."

"I know," Uncle Tim said, "but I've been thinking that if you come back for the spring semester, the school won't know what grade to put you in. It might be better if you waited until next fall."

"I want to come back now," I insisted.

"David says there are some good veterinary schools in Australia. You might even think about going to college in Sydney. Caitlin, are you still there?"

I put down the phone.

CHAPTER 25

Now History

No one was more surprised than I was when I won a prize for Australian history at Tennyson College. On Speech Night, I walked nervously across the stage in my white linen dress to accept the prize - a book - from the headmistress.

The students sat in rows in the refectory, and behind us were our proud parents. My dad and Enid were in the audience and they clapped enthusiastically.

"We are especially proud of Caitlin Pritchard," Miss Shock told the assembly. "She came to us from America only a few short months ago. Tonight, she has won the Fourth Form prize for Australian history over all her classmates."

Ann Engels won the prize for English again. The other girls gathered around us, offering their congratulations. "This time they gave me 'Jane Eyre,'" Ann said. "What book did you get, Caitlin?"

I had been too excited to notice. I looked down at the smooth, glossy cover. My prize was an illustrated history of the Hawkesbury Valley. A beautiful sketch of St. Matthew's Church graced the front cover. The book almost slipped out of my hands when I saw the name of the artist was Ainsley Allen.

To my surprise, Barry Egan-Smith was suddenly standing in front of me. "Hi, Caitlin," he said. "Didn't you know Brebner boys are always invited to Speech Night?"

"How are you, Barry?" Despite everything, I was pleased to see him.

"I'm all right," Barry said. "I thought I might have seen you at the school dances."

"I've been busy studying," I said.

"I think it is great that you won the history prize."

"It wasn't that difficult. I like history."

Barry held up his key chain, displaying a colored token. "I've joined a support group for teenagers with addictions. I've been 'clean' now for three months."

"Congratulations," I said.

"I think I've got the marks to go on to uni', by the way."

"I knew you could do it."

"Once I stopped being an idiot," he admitted. "I know you don't think much of me---."

"I just didn't like some of the things you were doing," I interrupted. "It doesn't matter about that.

I'm going to boarding school in Sydney next term."

"You are?"

I hesitated. Maybe it was time to face the idea. "My father is getting married again. He and Enid need some space."

"You won't be going back to America, will you?" Barry asked.

"I'm thinking about going to college---university in Australia."

"I'll probably be getting a flat - an apartment - in Sydney next year," Barry said. "If your school will let me, I could take you out at weekends - that is, if you want me to."

I smiled. "It would relieve the boredom."

"We might be at uni' together one day," Barry said, enthusiastically. He went on, "My mother has a time-share deal at Little Hartley. Have you been up there?"

I shook my head.

"It's an old farm in the Blue Mountains. If you like, we could drive up there on Saturday. Mum will be there. We could go horseback riding. They have some great trails."

"How old is it?"

Barry stared at me. "Pardon?"

"How old is the farm?"

"I don't know. Pretty old."

I sighed. Some day, I might have to tell Barry how I was about old houses.

That evening, I slipped out of the kitchen to the back garden. It was summer time and I slapped at mosquitoes buzzing around me as I went out to the vacant lot with Sebastian. In the dim light, I parted the branches of the weeping willow trees, remembering how Ainsley had liked this place. Smiling to myself, I kissed the cover of the book I had won at Speech Night before laying it carefully against the trunk of a tree. I knew Ainsley was gone, but I wanted to dedicate my prize to him, anyway. Somewhere, somehow, he might be watching.

As I walked back to the gate, I noticed Sebastian was looking past me to something in the vacant lot. I turned around and, for one brief moment, I thought I saw Ainsley standing by the willow tree. I took a step forward, my pulse beating in my throat. "Ainsley?"

Ainsley was beautifully dressed, with his blond hair in order and a silk cravat around his neck. He was smiling at me. "Thank you for the book, Caitlin. Thank you for everything. I was selfish to ask you to come with me before you had fulfilled your destiny."

I whispered, "You weren't selfish."

"Yes, I was. You still have to do your own 'thing,' as modern people say." His smile was wistful. "You see, I have been learning, too." He was holding out my digital watch. "'We hanged our harps upon the willows.' That is an old psalm. I thought you should have your watch back, since your mother gave it to you."

I blinked, making sure I was not hallucinating. "I don't need the watch."

"Nor do I," Ainsley said. "I have all the time in the world. But someone will soon be looking for you."

I said, quickly, "No one is looking for me."

"We waited centuries to be together," Ainsley said. "We can wait a little longer. I will remember you."

"Are you happy?" I stammered. "Where you are, I mean?"

"Of course. Take your watch. I had it inscribed for you."

Our hands touched briefly as Ainsley put the watch in my palm. I opened my mouth to speak, but before I could say anything else, he was gone. Instinctively, I looked up at the sky. The constellations were different from those I was used to in the northern hemisphere, but I thought I could

161

make out the Southern Cross like a beacon in the dark.

Under the porch light, I turned the watch over and read the words Ainsley had engraved on the back: "Time means naught to angels."

CHAPTER 26

To: "Dr. Tim Robbins" <timrob@onramp.net>

Subject: Family News

Aunt Natalie, Uncle Tim, Marybeth, Alicia, and Peter,

I hope you are all well. Surprise! I won the prize for history in my grade at Speech Night or Award Night.

As I told you on the phone, I won't be going back to Tennyson College next year. I am going to boarding school in Sydney. I still want to be a veterinarian, but I don't know whether I will be going to college here or back home.

I would like to have seen you at Christmas, but we can talk on the phone, can't we? Did I tell you Dad is closing the store over the summer break so that we can go on vacation to Queensland? He says it is a tropical paradise. After that, he and Enid are getting married. By the way, I have become very interested in art. I have also met a nice Aussie boy. His name is Barry. Love, Caitlin.

END

ABOUT THE AUTHOR

Jeanne McNamara grew up in Australia and now lives in Texas. She has been writing since she was eleven, and truly enjoys writing for young people. Though things have changed tremendously since she was a teen, she believes that some things have not changed at all. "The feelings are still the same - love and joy and sadness are still the same for everyone."

Because the author has a particular interest in Australia's unique history, the geography, place names and historical references in "Caitlin's Country" are all authentic.

18387243R00096

Made in the USA
San Bernardino, CA
13 January 2015